The Plymouth was ~~~~~~~~~~ when the Ford blocked its way. The driver pulled hard to the right but could not avoid slamming into the rear fender of the Ford.

Before Chamus or his two men in the Plymouth knew what was happening, Stone was out of his car, his .45 leveled at the three men inside.

"Kill the motherfucker!" Chamus screamed, his voice so high it sounded like a wounded animal.

Stone saw the passenger reach inside his coat. Without hesitating he pulled the trigger on his pistol and watched in horror as the glass shattered. The black man's face disappeared in an orgy of blood and bone as the slug entered him just above the nose and between the eyes. Stone whirled and fired one second later at the driver. This time the bullet entered the man's eye, and like an exploding red rose blew out his eyeball and brains at the same moment.

Holloway House Originals by Donald Goines

DOPEFIEND
WHORESON
BLACK GANGSTER
STREET PLAYERS
WHITE MAN'S JUSTICE,
    BLACK MAN'S GRIEF
BLACK GIRL LOST
CRIME PARTNERS
CRY REVENGE
DADDY COOL
DEATH LIST
ELDORADO RED
INNER CITY HOODLUM
KENYATTA'S ESCAPE
KENYATTA'S LAST HIT
NEVER DIE ALONE
SWAMP MAN

Special Preview of *Swamp Man*—page 221

KENYATTA'S LAST HIT

Donald Goines

HOLLOWAY HOUSE CLASSICS are published by

Kensington Publishing Corp.
119 West 40th Street
New York, NY 10018

First Holloway House Classics mass market printing: January 2008

International Standard Book Number 978-0-87067-944-5
Printed in the United States of America

10 9 8 7 6 5 4 3

www.kensingtonbooks.com

*Dedicated to
my mother, Myrtle Goines, who had confidence in
my writing ability.*

KENYATTA'S LAST HIT

1

THE LATE SUMMER WINDS were blowing hard in Los Angeles. The sky was clear, but the streets and alleyways were clouded with dust and debris. In South Central Los Angeles, the population elected to stay indoors, out of the blistering wind and heat. Compton Boulevard, Manchester Boulevard, the take-out chicken and taco stands, the old newsstand at the corner of Adams and Crenshaw, they were all dark and empty. The only sounds were those of the wind whistling eerily through the rotting buildings.

Elliot Stone felt the wind bite at his face. He walked, head down, along Compton, clutching the small packet of film tightly beneath his leather coat.

His six-foot-one frame moved smoothly as he ducked one gust after another. In his days at the University of Southern California, the young black man had worked his way through tougher obstacles than the Santa Ana winds.

As Stone passed the Pacific Club, he heard the mellow sounds of a Miles Davis record drifting out onto the street. The music lifted his spirits. The desolation on the streets was uncommon in Watts, and it was good to know that at least a few people were drinking and listening to the good sounds.

The small white house at the corner of Fifty-first street and Compton beckoned to Stone with its clean exterior and the familiar sign above the door that read: Office of Economic Opportunity, South Central Office.

For two years Stone had worked out of this office, helping his black brothers and sisters to achieve some kind of reasonable start in the community. As a former football star and student, the job had come easily to the well-mannered, soft-spoken black youth. The white bureaucracy liked their neighborhood representatives to be like Elliot Stone. It gave them the opportunity to bring the workers uptown to the Century Plaza Hotel or the Statler Hilton for conferences.

In the old days, men like H. Rap Brown and Eldridge Cleaver frightened off the soft, white businessmen from the Valley and Beverly Hills with their hate-filled rhetoric and powerful language. The days of poverty Mau-Mau were finished. No more were blacks intimidating the white man with their African garb and Dark Continent souls. It had worked for a number of years, but now the clean-cut, well-educated men like Elliot Stone were making the climb. And it was making life easier for the nervous white men who dealt with them.

The light was on inside the small house. Stone knew that Jimmy Adams and Frank Robinson would be huddled inside the back office, sorting out files and poring over photographs. Stone used his key, opened the front door, and made his way through the main front offices to the rear of the building.

"What's happenin', gentlemen?" Stone said brightly, smiling at the two older blacks sitting at the huge wood table.

Jimmy Adams, the older of the two men, sat beneath the naked white light, his bald head gleaming with perspiration, and smiled. "You got the photos, Elliot?" he asked.

Stone pulled out the packet of pictures, twenty-four four-by-four black-and-whites, and spread them out on the table. "Yes sir, we got somethin' happenin' here."

Frank Robinson, small, stocky, and with short hair, busied himself with the mass of paper and photographs remaining on the table. When he had scooped them all up into a pile, he turned his attention back to the series of snapshots that Stone had put before them.

Elliot Stone placed each of the photos side by side, then stood back and admired the collection. Each picture showed a black man standing outside a local bar named The Black Oasis. With him was another black man, an older, better dressed man, who possessed all the markings of a pimp.

"Now," Stone began softly, his two friends peering intently at the pictures, "we got them bastards together. The one on the right, as you know, is Wilbur Chamus. We got proof connecting him with the local ring at Manual Arts High School. Right, Jimmy?"

Adams nodded. "You can dig we got his ass, Elliot!"

"Beautiful. Now, we got this other dude. This cat has been making the scene down at the Oasis for three weeks. Each of these shots was taken on a Tuesday afternoon over a period of three months."

"Pull my coat, Elliot," Frank said excitedly. "Who is he?"

Elliot Stone smiled, revealing fine white teeth. "Well, gentlemen, the dude is named Oscar Manning."

There was a long silence. Jimmy Adams whistled through his teeth, then chuckled. "Oscar Manning…, man, that dude is somethin' else. Vegas, 'Frisco…, right?"

"You got it, Jimmy," Elliot replied. "Oscar Manning, according to those cats who should know, is the biggest fuckin' runner of heroin this side of the goddamn Rocky Mountains! An' we got him in black and white with Chamus."

Frank Robinson moved back a step from the table. Written across his hard, black face was worry. He had begun with Stone six months before, helping him collect and gather information on the local drug scene.

At that time, he had expected maybe one or two small-time high-school pushers. Oscar Manning, and even Chamus, were something a little heavier.

"You uptight, my man?" Elliot glared at Robinson. He had not disliked the man, just failed to respect him.

"Shit!" Robinson replied. "You fuckin' around in dangerous waters, Elliot. That dude's a heavy motherfucker!"

Stone chuckled. "An' so are we, Robinson."

"What we goin' to do now, Elliot?" Adams asked quickly, as a means of breaking the tension. Stone continued to glare at Robinson for a moment longer before turning his attention back to the photographs.

"Yeah," the tall black man said slowly "We put this shit together and take it to Kenyatta. Robinson is right. This shit is too big for just us. We been workin' with Kenyatta a long time, and now we got somethin' to show him."

The silence in the room was what Stone had anticipated. The name of Kenyatta brought that to the black brothers quickly. The man was a legend, and men do not speak of legends without taking the time to consider what they are going to say. That was the way it was with Kenyatta.

That night Stone had sat alone inside his small office and thought deeply about what he was doing. His record in the office was a good one. But the situation around him was deteriorating quickly. The young people, all blacks, were being taken for a ride, a cruise on drugs from which they would not return. And the little white man who held the power had told him nothing more than any other bureaucratic slave would have.

It had taken one phone call by Stone to arrange the meeting with the man they called Kenyatta. Stone had heard of him on the streets. There was a growing number of young, idealistic blacks who had joined with the tall, bald-headed black man. They had known that the government, the law enforcement agencies, and the supposed poverty programs were not working. Kenyatta had told them that the situation was in their hands, that they were the force behind the ghetto, and that they would be the ones who could make it better for their brothers.

Kenyatta arrived at the office with two bodyguards, a black man named Wells and a short, stocky black named Burt.

Stone and Kenyatta had retreated to the back room of the small house and talked through the night. During their discussion, they had organized an extensive campaign of information gathering that they both hoped would mean the destruction of the drug trade in Watts. Using the OEO office as a front, the two men had agreed to work hand in hand in an attempt to locate the pushers, the traffickers, and the users. Once that information was completed, they would then move in and use whatever force was necessary to smash the ring.

Now, one year later, Stone was in a position to give Kenyatta the information he needed. The largest ring in Watts was sitting in front of him, captured in a series of photographs and documents collected from the street people. All told, the three black men sitting in the rear of the OEO office had collected more than a hundred pages and five hundred photographs depicting the drug trade in the area. That information a year ago would have been handed over to the local authorities, or possibly the FBI. But Stone was geared to the Kenyatta philosophy now, and he knew what had to be done.

Jimmy Adams leaned back in his chair with the small stack of photos in front of him. "We should lock these up till Kenyatta picks 'em up."

Stone nodded, then walked to the far wall and pulled open a slab of wall paneling. Behind the grained wood was a small box with a lock. Stone pulled out a key and opened the box. Adams handed him the photographs and Stone placed them inside the box along with a series of documents.

"The rest of that shit," Stone said, pointing to the massive collection of papers and photos on the table, "should be filed. What we got in this damn box is enough for Kenyatta."

Robinson began gathering the stacks of papers and putting them into the large file cabinet in the corner of the room.

"You goin' call Kenyatta?" Adams asked.

"That's been taken care of, my man. We're meeting in an hour." Stone grinned. After months of frustrations, his efforts were finally paying off. Tonight he would meet again with the man who held the real power—a rising ghetto king with the idealism, along with the force, to make a difference.

"Hey, Frank," Jimmy asked, "ain't we got ourselves a bottle of Jack Daniels in that cabinet?"

Robinson reached inside the top drawer and pulled out a fifth. There was more than half left in the bottle. "Now," Robinson said, unscrewing the cap, "that's what I call valuable records!"

The three men laughed and began passing the bottle as they talked of their accomplishments.

The large, black Ford pulled to a stop in front of the OEO building. The four young black men sat inside staring at the small white house.

The driver, a tall, lanky youth with a huge Afro and darkly tinted shades, turned to his companions. "Looks like the motherfuckers are in the back," he said.

The wind ripped at the car and shook it. The tension inside was tremendous. All four men were sweating and breathing heavily. Finally, the driver opened his door and stepped out into the hot wind.

His three companions joined him. Each man held a sawed-off shotgun at his side. Beneath their leather jackets was the familiar bulge of a shoulder holster, complete with snub-nosed .38s. On the back of the jackets a picture of a black man with a huge Afro and tinted sunglasses was painted between the arms of crossed bones. Above that, in dripping red blood lettering, was the name "The Black Maria."

"What you think, Curt," the smallest of the four asked the driver. "We make it through the back?"

"No way," Curt replied. "We goin' in straight ahead

and blast these cats to hell 'fore they know what hit
'em!"

Curt's small gang stood upright and tense. Each
man gripped his shotgun with force. "All right…, let's
go," Curt said after a long silence.

Elliot Stone had just handed the bottle of Jack
Daniels to Jimmy when he thought he heard the front
door creak open. Dismissing the concern, he blamed
the noise on the howling wind. But as Jimmy raised
the bottle to his lips, Stone heard the footsteps outside in the main office. Before he could turn around,
the door was kicked in. The four black, Afroed men
of the Black Maria stood facing Stone and his partners. The shotguns were pointed directly at them.

"Now," Curt began in a voice which revealed the
tension he was feeling, "you motherfuckers just stay
where you are. Any of you Jacks makes a move, I'll
personally see to it that your fuckin' head disappears!"

Stone was standing behind the table, the farthest
one from Curt and the other three. To his right, Jimmy
was sitting at the table, the bottle of whiskey still
raised to his mouth. Only now, the brown liquid was
pouring out of the bottle and onto his shirt and
trousers. To his left, Frank was leaning against the file
cabinet. His legs appeared as though they would buck-
le at any time. At that moment, Stone knew there was
no chance.

"We hear you dudes been collecting a little info on
some cat's activities hereabouts. That the straight?"
Curt glared first at Frank, then at Jimmy, and finally
turned his baleful stare upon Stone.

"Hey, dude," Curt said coldly, "I ain't fuckin' 'round, man. You dig where I'm comin' from?"

"Yeah," Stone managed to say, "but I don't know what kind of jive you handin' down, brother."

Suddenly, Jimmy spoke up. His voice was tinged with his fear. "Please, man. We got some shit…right here…."

Curt grinned, his lips spreading across crooked, stained teeth. "Now, this little dude got some smarts, baby."

Stone watched as Jimmy picked up the file envelopes on the table, then walked across the room and pulled the one that Frank had just put away. He turned and handed the folders to Curt.

"Any more shit like this?" Curt asked as he quickly glanced at the materials.

"No, man," Jimmy claimed, "this is all the shit. I mean that."

Curt laughed, then nodded to the smallest of the gang. He in turn pulled out a can of black spray paint, then walked to the far wall and wrote the name of the gang in large, sprawling letters.

Stone watched, and the name "Black Maria" rang a bell. It had been a gang operating out of the Manual Arts High School. A bunch of young toughs who had done nothing worse with their activities than ripping off a few cars and dealing in reds and grass. As far as Stone had seen, they were never into anything as heavy as killing.

"You dudes look a little old…," Stone said after the small black man had finished his lettering.

"Old for what, motherfucker?" Curt retorted sharply.

"The Maria's..., they're high-school kids, you dig?"

Curt laughed sardonically. "Don't believe nothin' you ever hear or see, 'cause you'll live a lot longer. I guess for you, man, the time is too short anyway. Too fuckin' bad you never had a chance to practice my advice...."

Stone watched in horror as Curt raised his gun and pointed the barrel directly at Stone's stomach. The former football star felt himself tighten involuntarily, the same way he had done on the gridiron when he saw a two-hundred-and-sixty-pound giant ready to take off his head.

The room was filled with a deadening silence. The four men with guns stood with their weapons pointing directly at the three unarmed men. All time, all movement seemed suspended. Even the wind, which had been howling only moments before, calmed into a gentle, stilling breeze.

The four shotguns fired at the same time, as though the moment of the killing had been rehearsed. Jimmy was hit directly in the face. Blood spurted from his eyes as the sockets were ruptured by the splattering of pellets from the shell. The rest of his face, except for his mouth, was blown away in an orgy of blood and skin. Jimmy's mouth was formed into a grotesque, horrified grimace.

Frank was belted from the side and into the head. Two shotguns had been trained on him, and each got him squarely. Where his left temple and ear had once been there now existed only a gaping hole, and the oozing brain matter that quickly moved out of his dying body and onto the floor. He had been plastered against the filing cabinets, and his body remained in a prone position.

Curt fired at Elliot, aiming for the man's crotch. But the pellets hit him in the stomach and punched a series of holes into his gut. The blood was oozing out quickly, staining Elliot's white shirt. The force of the blast had thrown him back against the rear door, and Stone fell to a heap on the floor.

The room was filled with the blue-gray smoke of the explosions. The crumpled bodies were barely visible to Curt. "Okay…, set it," Curt ordered, his eyes burning from the dense sulphur fumes.

The two men who had fired at Frank quickly grabbed some papers and newspapers and began lighting them. They threw the wadded-up fireballs across the room and into other stacks of paper. Within a moment, the room was crowded with small fires that would soon burst into huge, smoldering flames.

On their way through the house to the front door, the four members of the Black Maria set fire to anything that would ignite easily—chairs, paper, and tesks. By the time they reached the door, the entire house behind them was quickly being engulfed in flames.

At first, Elliot Stone could not differentiate between the fire in his gut and fire all around him. The pain that engulfed him was more intense than any fire could be.

"Oh God…, Jesus…," Stone cried when he managed to clear the tears away from his eyes. He saw through the smoke and flames the butchered bodies of Jimmy and Frank. Then he felt the flames licking at the bottom of his pants.

Stone's instinct took over. Years of athletic training had geared his muscles into action, without even being aware of it. Instantly, the young black man began crawling with all the strength he possessed toward the back door. It was only a distance of five feet, but it felt like an eternity. His survival instinct pushed him on, yet the pain, combined with the intense heat of the room, caused him to black out. When he regained consciousness, he pushed again, not knowing anymore why he was going or where. The door had been a reality only moments before. But now, it was part of a nightmare.

The flames were surrounding him on all sides. The bottom of his pants were burning, and the flames were moving up. Elliot Stone reached up and grabbed the door handle. He twisted it. But the heat of the fire had melted the metal, and the handle was jammed.

He knew he had one last chance, one last effort to make, and then everything would be decided. "Goddamn!" Stone cried as he staggered to his feet. Without looking, or even being able to see, he moved back away from the door, then bent over and clutched his stomach. He was in the position of receiving a handoff from the quarterback.

The autumn day was bright and cheerful. One hundred thousand crazed fans yelled as one in the Los

Angeles Memorial Coliseum. Before him, the huge front line of Notre Dame moved together, darkening the skies and making it impossible to see the end zone.

But at that moment, Elliot Stone bent down, clutched the football to his gut, and somehow managed to plow his way through the world's biggest college line and into the end zone. He was mobbed by his teammates and by the students who were pouring *en masse* out of the stands. In his entire life, the young black athlete had never felt so happy to be alive.

There were no teammates mobbing Elliot Stone as he writhed in pain on the cool grass behind the inferno of the OEO building. Instead, he was alone with his pain and his wounds. The fire was out on his pants, and his hands could feel the blood oozing out of his belly.

But at least he was still alive.

2

KENYATTA HELD THE telephone tightly in his hand. His black brow was rippled with concern, his dark eyes turned cold and hard. "The OEO office has been hit," he said softly.

The two other men in the living room stared at the floor. Neither was able to handle the rage that emanated from the big black man who sat on the couch. Both Edgar and Rufus had known Kenyatta long enough to know when words were worthless.

"They were hit by a gang, the Black Maria's. The name was painted across the outside of the fuckin' house!" Kenyatta replaced the receiver, raised his large frame off the couch and walked quickly to the bar. "They burned every motherfuckin' file inside. Everything."

Finally Edgar spoke up. "Did they get everyone? I mean, Jimmy and Frank and Elliot?"

Kenyatta poured out three shots of Jack Daniels and handed a glass to each of his partners. The two men accepted the drinks gratefully. "Don't know, Edgar," Kenyatta began after taking a long swallow of the whiskey. "My man Steve out there laid it down to me. Ambulances, fire department, and cops. He couldn't tell if any of the brothers survived."

Rufus looked intently at Kenyatta. Already the strong man's bald head was glistening with sweat. Rufus knew that Kenyatta did not sweat unless he was reaching the boiling point. "You all right, Kenyatta?" Rufus asked.

Kenyatta shrugged, then poured another round. "Yeah, I'm okay, Rufus. It's just that we were so fuckin' close. Elliot was excited, man. Laid down some talk 'bout havin' the drug thing tied up. We were close, my man. Very close."

The three men drank in silence. Kenyatta's mind took him back to the first time he had met Elliot Stone. It had been at the same office of the OEO, and Kenyatta had gone there to try to straighten out some problems for his people. Stone had been the man to help him, and Kenyatta had been impressed with the young man's honesty and courage.

Normally, whenever Kenyatta had "hit" a federal project, he was able to instill enough fear into the people that all his demands were met. But with Stone,

Kenyatta had met a match. From that day on, Kenyatta had made a concerted effort at recruiting the ex-footballer into his rapidly growing organization.

He had failed over and over again until that cold January night when Stone had called him. That had been the beginning. Since then, Kenyatta had worked closely with Stone, giving the younger man everything he knew in the way of experience and ability. With Stone's intelligence and youth, Kenyatta had envisioned the younger man as a son, someone who would carry on his fight after he was gone.

And now, Kenyatta did not know whether Elliot Stone was alive or was resting in eternity as a pile of scorched marrow and flesh inside the building.

"Man," Kenyatta began coldly, breaking the long silence, "we got to hit whoever was responsible for this shit. We got to hit those motherfuckers so bad! No way any dude who had anything to do with this is goin' be walking around alive after we finish."

"Tha's all we got, right now," Edgar agreed. "We got to do somethin'."

The drink, now a third round, was raising the fire in their blood. Each man had lost something in the hit. Besides their devotion to Kenyatta and his goal of cleaning out the community, both Edgar and Rufus had lost old friends. Jimmy and Frank had been with them for a long time. It was a difficult thing to let a friend die without making someone pay for it. And both men's minds were quickly being set in that direction.

"All right," Kenyatta began. "I want to start this shit

right now. You, Edgar, you get everyone together from
Compton and Lynwood. Rufus, you take care of all
the members in Watts and downtown."

Rufus and Edgar nodded.

"And," Kenyatta continued, "any information either
of you dudes connects on, you just bring it to me without tellin' no one. You dig?"

"We'll keep it down, Kenyatta," Edgar replied,
answering for both men as he normally did.

Kenyatta moved from behind the mahogany bar and
crossed the lush living room of his apartment. In the
past, the rich wood furnishings and thickly carpeted
floor gave the man much pleasure. His wall-to-wall
stereo, his twenty-five-inch color television, all of it
had served to keep him mellow and happy. But now,
none of these things mattered. All the big man could
think about was Elliot Stone.

General Hospital on a Saturday night in Los
Angeles resembled something close to the battlefields
of Europe during World War II. Stretchers lined the
inner lobby, white-coated doctors rushed back and
forth, while nurses and orderlies rushed around madly.
The only difference between the battlefields of
Hitler's war and General Hospital was the color of the
wounded. Every man, woman, and child awaiting
treatment in the mammoth hospital on this windy
Saturday night was black.

Elliot Stone had been picked up, screaming and
writhing on the lawn behind the OEO office, by the
Los Angeles Fire Department. After giving the seri-

ously wounded man emergency medical care, they took him to County General. He was rushed into the emergency receiving ward, an expanse of partitioned cubicles separated only by curtains. The cries of pain and fear emanating from each sector gave the low-ceilinged room an aura of death.

Stone was taken into cubicle number nineteen, a small sector at the far end of the room next to the plasma stands and the shelves that contained bottles of blood. Two interns quickly attended to the wounded black, ripping off his shirt and beginning what would become a long series of attempts to stop the bleeding.

It was quickly decided by the attending doctor that an operation was needed immediately. The shotgun pellets had penetrated the lining of Stone's stomach, and internal bleeding was at a dangerous level. Calling for an intern, the doctor moved downstairs where the operation would be conducted.

Joe Collins moved quickly to the site of Elliot Stone's bed and began making preparations to transport him to the operating room. The young black intern was efficient and quick. He had learned his job well and did not have to stop and think as he attached the plasma line to the portable roller and made the entire system mobile.

The black man lying on the bed with first-degree burns and a shattered belly was just one more in a continuing series of dark-skinned brothers Joe Collins had attended to that night. He was one more body on the verge of death brought to the hospital from the battlefield of the ghettos.

The bed was ready, and Joe Collins called for another intern to help move Stone across the floor and to the elevator. As the young intern waited, he looked down at the man on the bed for the first time. Recognition dawned on Collins quickly. Every man in Kenyatta's organization was required to memorize the names and faces of every other member. It was a condition that Kenyatta demanded from his people.

The other intern arrived and helped Collins push the bed through the crowded, massive ward and into the elevator. Once inside, the orderly, a white youth, looked at Collins. "He a friend? You look worried," he said.

Collins shrugged. "No, man. Just seeing a brother comin' in like this...."

"Happens so much you'd think you were used to it by now."

"Yeah. But sometimes it gets heavy. Kind of drives one into the gut, you know?" Collins turned to the doors as the elevator stopped. The operating room was another massive room, sectioned off with nurses and interns running crazily from one area to the next, carrying plasma bottles, freshly sterilized equipment, and medical charts. Ten doctors were working this area— five more than usual because it was a Saturday night.

A nurse approached the elevator and directed Collins toward an empty sector. A white-haired doctor stood waiting behind the curtain. He watched the body of another nameless black man as Elliot Stone was wheeled into his room.

"This boy's got it bad, nurse," the doctor shouted.

"We'll do an exploratory first!"

Suddenly the small partitioned room was filled with nurses and two interns. They began stripping Stone's body and injecting him with massive doses of sodium pentothal. Collins watched for another minute, then walked away.

Upstairs, Collins went to his supervisor, an elderly woman with a crisp and efficient manner. He asked her if he could get some coffee. She frowned at him, then agreed to let him take his break an hour ahead of schedule.

The hospital cafeteria was on the fourth floor. A huge, dreary room with scattered tables colored brightly to eliminate the tension and depression that most people were feeling inside. Collins grabbed a cup of coffee and walked across the room toward the far end. There he stepped into a telephone booth and dialed the number that he had memorized, yet had never used.

Collins waited for three rings before someone answered. "It is a cold, windy night in Detroit," Collins said quickly.

"How cold?" the voice on the other end asked softly.

"'Bout twenty-five degrees and snowing."

The man on the other end put the phone down and within a few seconds it was picked up again. "Yes?" the voice on the other end asked.

Collins breathed a sigh of relief when he recognized Kenyatta's voice. He had not spoken with the man for over three months, but Kenyatta's deep coldness was always apparent. "Man," Collins began, speaking softly, "I have news here at County General."

"Go ahead, Collins," Kenyatta replied, his voice
betraying something akin to excited anticipation.

Before he spoke again, Collins allowed the momen-
tary flash of excitement to flood his mind. Kenyatta
had remembered him, had remembered his name.
Collins took a deep breath before speaking again.
"They have brought in Elliot Stone," he said.

"Yes, go ahead," Kenyatta replied, no longer careful to hide his excitement.

"The man's got first-degree burns and massive internal wounds. But the doc thinks he'll make it. They're
operating right now."

"Thanks, my man," Kenyatta said with relief. "I
want information as soon as it comes down, dig? I'll
leave this line open."

"Right. No sweat," Collins replied.

"And Collins," Kenyatta began, "you got to get
yourself prepared for any kind of shit. You dig where
I'm comin' from?"

"Yeah," Collins replied. "Anythin', man, anythin' at
all."

"Good," Kenyatta replied, then hung up the phone.

Collins stood in the phone booth for a moment
longer, feeling the surge of respect and power. He had
talked with the big man, had given him information
that had obviously concerned him. Collins had long
been a believer in Kenyatta and in his ideals and goals.
To be in a position to help him had been one of Joe
Collins' goals in life. Apparently, the man Elliot Stone
was an important link in Kenyatta's organization.

And right now, he was at the mercy of the police and the hospital authorities. Only one contact existed between Stone and Kenyatta, and that man was Joe Collins.

Kenyatta's woman, Betty, was at the apartment within ten minutes of his call. She had been with friends, relaxing and enjoying her Saturday night, when the phone call had come. Immediately, without hesitation, the tall, dark-skinned woman had run to her man.

"Listen, honey," Kenyatta began in an excited voice, "we got to get somethin' set up here."

Betty looked toward Edgar and Rufus. Both men stood next to the bar. Their faces were intent.

"Elliot Stone's place was hit tonight," Kenyatta continued, "an' he's in General Hospital now. They're operatin'. He was hit real bad."

"Oh, baby, I'm sorry," Betty replied. She had known how Kenyatta felt about Stone. Many times after they had made love, Kenyatta would smoke a cigarette and talk about the plans he had for Stone within his organization. Betty had liked Stone very much, but there was something about him that had stirred a fear or apprehension deep inside her.

The man, Betty thought, knew too much, was too well educated. She had been with Kenyatta since the early days in Detroit and was used to the black man's rage and clear thinking. But Kenyatta had always acted on instinct and had always acted directly.

"Now," Kenyatta began in a soft voice, "we got to

get some friends of yours in here who know some-thin' 'bout nursing. We goin' get our man out of that fuckin' death trap and bring him here!"

Betty waited for a second before replying. "Are you sure, baby? I mean, if he's hurt bad as you say, shouldn't we let him stay there where they can take care of him?"

Kenyatta chuckled. "Baby, you got 'nough common sense to know what kind of shit goes down in those motherfuckin' places. Did you know that, in Detroit last year, over half the dudes brought into the General Hospital didn't have to die? They were fucked over, treated badly, and shitted on!"

Kenyatta paused for a moment, lighting a cigarette and looking at the three people in the room. "An' all of those dudes," Kenyatta continued, "were blacks."

"Jesus," Rufus moaned.

"That's right, brother," Kenyatta replied. "All fuckin' blacks the city don't give enough of a damn about. You see that kind of action goin' down out there in those motherfuckin' white suburbs? Ain't no way."

Betty looked at her man quietly and with admira-tion. She could never stop respecting him. Even though he wasn't educated like Elliot Stone, he still managed to know what had to be known. "Okay, baby," she said softly, "I'll get Sarah and Beatrice. Both of 'em were registered nurses. But what you goin' do about a doctor?"

Kenyatta smiled. "Taken care of, Betty. Remember that dude in Compton who almost lost his license because of the abortions? Well, he's more than willin' to repay ol' Kenyatta for the favor I done him."

"And equipment," Rufus chimed in excitedly, "he's bringing all the shit we need. We're goin' make a fuckin' hospital out of this place!"

Kenyatta laughed. "Man, if we let Stone sit around that death house for more than twelve hours, we'd be giving three different groups a chance to nail him. If the dudes who hit the house didn't, then the fuckin' police would be all over him. And if none of those two motherfuckers did him in, the fuckin' hospital would find a way!"

Everyone in the room was silent for a moment. Betty continued to stare at her man with love in her eyes. Rufus and Edgar stared at their man with respect and determination.

"All right," Kenyatta said finally, "let's get this shit started. We're goin' pull Elliot out of there soon as they finish patchin' him up."

Rufus and Edgar smiled. Kenyatta was going to take every precaution, do everything necessary to see to it that Elliot Stone got back alive. The two Kenyatta men would devote themselves completely to carrying out the man's orders that night. They both knew that Kenyatta always worked this way and that sometime during their lifetime they might need the same kind of action.

It was the kind of thing that made Kenyatta's band of men strongly united. It was the kind of thing that allowed Kenyatta to possess the kind of power that he had.

3

IT WAS A HOT AND MUGGY night in Detroit. The moisture poured off Lake St. Clair, and mixing with the heat from the plains to the southwest, it created an almost unbearable kind of steambath.

Detectives Ed Benson and Jim Ryan cruised slowly down Fifty-first Street checking out the old, dilapidated storefronts and iron-gated liquor stores.

"We've been looking for this dude for three days," Ryan said to his black partner.

Benson nodded, pulled out a cigarette, and peered across the steering wheel at a darkly shrouded storefront. For a moment he thought he saw a figure crouching in the shadows, but on a second look, he realized it was his eyes playing games with him. "Yeah, Ryan," Benson replied. "It's been a shit-ass assignment. One lousy junkie terrorizing the whole damn southside, and we got to find him!"

Three long nights of prowling the neighborhood in their unmarked car searching through every known hangout in town had provided the two detectives with nothing more than strained nerves. The change in routine, the drabness of their search had been a complete reversal of what the two detectives had been used to in the past. Eleven months had passed since the holocaust at Kenyatta's ranch, a virtual slaughter that had culminated in a mass of dead black men and three white police officers losing their lives.

In the entire history of the Detroit Police Department there had never been anything like it. It had come to be referred to as the "farm country massacre" by the press and the local citizens.

That had been one of the closest chances Benson and Ryan had ever come to the fabled Kenyatta. The elusive leader of blacks from the ghetto had somehow escaped, hijacked a plane, and crash-landed in the vast desert outside Las Vegas. From that moment on, he had virtually disappeared off the face of the earth.

But then information started filtering in. Information that gave good reason to believe Kenyatta and the remains of his vengeful band had made it to Los Angeles. And Benson and Ryan, who had been on his tail virtually from the beginning—a beginning that had included two small-time killers named Billy and Jackie, and even the murderous drug pusher

Kingfisher—were chosen to track him down.

Who else, their captain had reasoned, knew more about the elusive Kenyatta than Benson and Ryan. And so they agreed to assist the FBI and the LAPD.

Kenyatta, Betty, Eddie-Bee, Jug, Jeannie, and the dying Red were headed for Watts in two separate cars when they had to stop for gas. A police cruiser pulled into the station and Red, crazed in his near-death state, jumped from the car and started shooting.

Benson and Ryan were already headed to the area, which in the meantime had turned into a hellish inferno of death when a stray bullet had struck a gas pump.

In a last-minute dash for life, Kenyatta drove his car through the service area of the station and through to the other side, just as Benson's and Ryan's car rounded the corner. Too late the black and white detective team realized that they had missed their best chance to nab the fabled Kenyatta. Then they were requested to return home.

Benson and Ryan had pleaded with their captain for an assignment to track Kenyatta through the Southwest and West. But their request had been denied. The two men were sent back onto regular duty, dealing with the pimps, the junkies, and the pushers. It seemed as though the man who had become an obsession to both detectives would never again faze their lives.

Now, Benson and Ryan drove through the empty streets of Detroit. In another two hours the sun would rise and stifling heat would begin to curse the ghetto. The two detectives would leave their shift, grab a quick, greasy breakfast, and fall into bed for another attempt at eight hours of sleep.

Benson listened to the police radio as he smoked his cigarette. He reached for the phone when he heard his call letters and picked it up. "Benson here," he said.

"The captain asks that you report to headquarters immediately," the girl on the other end said matter-of-factly.

"Yeah, be right in." Benson replaced the phone and looked at his partner. "Wonder what the old bastard wants now."

"Probably got us a fifteen-year-old junkie who's turnin' in his brother as a pusher." There was no mistaking the bitterness in Ryan's voice.

The police building was dark and depressing. The old brick structure had been standing for more than fifty years. The joke around the headquarters was that when the building celebrated its fiftieth year they would condemn it. That never happened. The city was running low on funds because of the automobile shutdowns. Even Tiger Stadium, where the Lions and Tigers played their games, had not been renovated, and that would normally take first priority.

Captain Frank Turner waited inside his small, cluttered office for the two detectives. The small, rotund senior officer clenched a cigar tightly between his teeth. He held two manila folders containing sheets that had come over the wire service. His pudgy face was wrinkled into a position of serious thought when

Detectives Benson and Ryan entered his office.

"Have a seat, gentlemen," Turner growled behind the thick cigar. Benson looked quickly at Ryan and knew that his partner was thinking the same thing. A chewing-out from Turner normally began with the old, gruffy captain having the men remain standing. Serious business was conducted from the civil position of sitting in chairs. At least, thought Benson, the old bastard has something worthwhile instead of the usual complaints.

"How you boys been?" Turner began, shuffling the folders on the desk in front of him.

"Fine, Captain," Benson replied, wanting really to describe the boredom and uselessness that their job had come to represent but thinking better of it.

"That's good," Turner said blankly. Then the small captain stood up behind his desk and spread the folders out on the table. He leaned forward and looked at both men.

"Gentlemen," Turner began, "we've just gotten a wire-service report from Los Angeles. At approximately midnight last night an office of the OEO was attacked and burned to the ground by members of a teenage gang known as the Black Maria. One man named Elliot Stone somehow escaped and is now at County General. He was the head of the office."

Turner paused a moment, then bent down as if to reread the print on the reports. He looked up again at the two waiting detectives. "Two other men died at that fire, their bodies burned beyond recognition. But the teeth remained, and the L.A. police were able to get a print. They have been identified as Jimmy Adams and Frank Robinson. Ring a bell'?"

Benson could feel the tension rise in the room. His partner leaned forward in his chair and let out a slow, impressive whistle.

"Well?" Turner asked.

"Kenyatta," Benson answered simply.

"Right. Both men, we believe, were in the massacre out at the farm. Now, they've turned up at the OEO in Los Angeles." Turner had not been on the force at the time of the Kenyatta massacre but had heard every variation of the story that existed. The hatred for the black leader that existed in Detroit was beyond anything that Turner had ever seen. He had been in New York when Malcolm X was alive and running meetings at the Garden, but the feelings were nothing like what existed within the Detroit Police Department.

It would be a feather in the cap of the longtime policeman if he could pay back the black man for the deaths within the department that he had caused.

Benson leaned back in his chair and watched the captain closely. He could see the anxiety and the excitement that he was feeling. But Benson was a black cop, contradiction within itself, and he had felt the pain and horror during the massacre when the tanks had been brought in. Those were his people, a bloodline that went deep into the darkest past of Africa, who were being shot and killed that day by a virtual army of policemen.

"You want Kenyatta?" Benson asked simply.

"Yes, I do," Turner replied, his voice slightly

shocked with anticipation. Already within the little captain's mind he could see the headlines, the adulation of the white community and the respect that he would garner from the rest of the department.

Jim Ryan stood up and walked to Turner's desk. "Captain, since that day, I've wanted nothing more than to nail that sonofabitch. I'm sure everyone in this damn building feels exactly the same way!"

Turner smiled and extended his hand to Ryan. But out of the corner of his eye, he was looking at Benson, who remained seated. "Thank you, Ryan. There's still a debt to be paid, and I think you're the man to collect."

Benson could not stop himself. The anger and the bitterness that had been building up inside like a volcano finally erupted. "Wait a second," Benson yelled, leaping from his chair. "Those people paid enough already. They paid with their lives. Women, children, and ten times the number of men killed on the force. They paid when we brought in those goddamn tanks and bazookas as if we were fighting some fucking foreign enemy!"

Ryan and Turner still clutched hands. Their faces told of their shock at Benson's outburst. Turner was afraid, but Ryan understood very well his partner's feelings. At that moment, he hated himself for having jumped to Turner like he had.

"Detective Benson," Turner said, his voice uneven, "those people out there that day *were* the enemy. We weren't dealing with a Martin Luther King or even a Malcolm X out there. We were dealing with a madman and his army of goddamn nig...."

Turner stopped himself quickly. "Negroes, Benson, who were trying to take over the damn city!"

Benson breathed deeply. There was nothing more he could say. Right now, his words could only be delivered through his fists, which rested clenched and threateningly next to his body.

"Listen, Ed," Ryan began in a soothing voice, "we all know how you felt about what happened out there that day. A lot of other people felt the same way. But you know better than most people just how Kenyatta works. It wasn't a racial thing, man, it was a police action."

"Now you listen, my man," Benson began coldly. "We know of ten, maybe fifteen goddamn 'super-patriot' white groups hanging around the outskirts of this city with enough of an arsenal to blow up the fuckin' town and the lake, too! The Minutemen, Sons of the Pioneers, Freedom Fighters...."

"But," Turner interrupted, "they're patriots, Benson. Men who fear the enemy and have attempted to prepare themselves for our protection. They don't want to overthrow the country. They want to save it!"

"They're still illegal, Captain. But we never go after them, do we?" Benson flinched, felt the adrenalin shoot through him and his body tense. He had gone too far, and yet he had not gone far enough.

Turner glared at Benson, then turned his back. He could see the rage in the large black man's body, and he feared it. The cords of Benson's neck were throbbing, his jaw muscles were tightened. The little white captain had seen enough of "them" when they were angry to know when to get out of the way.

"Now, listen," Turner began quietly, sitting behind his desk for the first time, "we're civilized men dealing with a professional problem here. Benson, you've brought up some good points, but they're irrelevant to the case at hand."

Benson saw the man creeping steadily into the womb of his position, retreating from him behind his gold badge. "All right, Captain," Benson said. "I am a professional and you are my immediate supervisor." The bitterness in his voice was not missed by Ryan.

"Captain," Ryan began in earnest, "we want this assignment. My partner feels strongly about it. He maybe feels too strongly."

Benson looked at Ryan and saw the man doing everything in his power to pull him out. Ryan was right. Benson was a professional, a black who many years before had given up his right to deal with the problem of race outside the law. It was his commitment and no one else's. At that time, Benson had believed in the system. Had seen, or thought he saw, the routes through which he could make a difference.

He knew that if those routes were closed to him, then all he had to do was to hand in his badge and make that journey to the twilight arena on the fringe. It was there that some of his brothers believed that out of the anarchy and chaos would come order and equality. But Benson, detective with the Detroit Police Department and black man, did not think so.

"Okay," Turner began quietly. "Enough of this dis-

cussion. Benson, I know how you feel and why. But
let's let that pass. Right now, we have more important things to discuss."

Benson looked at Ryan, then sat down in his chair.
Turner waited until both men were seated before talking. "You'll grab the first plane out of here for Los
Angeles. A Los Angeles detective, in charge of
narcotics and the general Watts area, will meet you
both at the airport. His name is Julius Stein, a good
man...."

Turner hesitated. He was going to add the phrase
"even though he's a kike," but Benson's dark, brood-
ing face had stopped him. "You should," he continued after clearing his throat, "have the complete coop-
eration of the LAPD."

"What about this guy Stone?" Ryan asked, leaning
forward again with that intense interest he always displayed at such meetings.

"Stone's at County, as I told you. According to our
reports, he's been hit badly in the stomach with a shotgun, and he's also suffering from first-degree burns
on his legs. The doctors are probably operating right
now."

Benson had calmed down enough to begin using his
professional mind once again. He sifted through his
memory, sorting out names, running down the cate-
gories of black men whom he had reason to be familiar with. The name Elliot Stone finally came to the
forefront. "Elliot Stone," he said, "wasn't he the running back at USC?"

Turner smiled. "That's right. Goddamn, he was a

good boy. Would've broken O.J.'s record 'cept for that injury. Shit, what a fuckin' runner!"

Benson smiled. It was always startling to him how white men could be so fond of "niggers"—as long as they were carrying a football, shooting a basket, or whacking a home run. Take them off the playing field and suddenly they're threats to society.

"Wonder what he was doing there," Ryan mused.

"He was pretty active," Benson replied. "Even when he was carrying the football. NAACP, worked a while for McGovern—an involved dude. It isn't surprising he was made head of that office so soon. The kid was bright."

"Well," Turner interjected, "that should make it all the more easy for you guys to get something out of him. If he's as bright as you say and knows anything about Kenyatta, he should be more than willing to help."

Benson was about to tell Turner that somehow that line of reasoning did not jive. A lot of bright young black men had gone Kenyatta's way because they were able to see what was really coming down. And that was where a man like Kenyatta pulled his strength. Instead, Benson mumbled something like, "I sure do hope so, Captain."

Turner nodded, then stood up and waddled around to the front of his desk. He passed Ryan and greeted Benson with an outstretched hand. "Benson," he began, pumping the black detective's hand too vigorously, "if there's any man in this department who has the talent to get something done out there, it's you."

"Thank you, sir," Benson said, playing the little charade through to the end. All he wanted now was to get out, get on that plane with Ryan, and begin using his skills to find out what was going down in Los Angeles.

After shaking Ryan's hand, Captain Turner gave each man a copy of the report and then told them to pick up the files on Kenyatta downstairs. He led the two men to the door and held it open for them. "I want a report filed out of L.A. every day. Set it up as soon as you arrive, and get to that damn hospital quick!"

Turner watched the two detectives walk down the hallway, then disappear around the corner. He closed the door to his office and sighed. He could feel his high blood pressure rising. Attempting to calm himself, he took a few deep breaths and exhaled quickly. His head was reeling from the confrontation with Benson. If the man hadn't been a fuckin' nigger, he said to himself, I would have had his ass back on the streets!

But Captain Turner wanted Kenyatta very badly, and he knew that, by using a black detective, his chances were that much greater. Turner had always been of the opinion that "those people" thought differently than white folks. Only a "nigger" could hope to understand another "nigger." Yes, thought Turner, now smiling to himself, it would take a nigger like Benson to nail a nigger like Kenyatta.

Satisfied with his decision, Captain Frank Turner snuggled into his leather-upholstered chair and leaned back. He would be off duty in another hour, and then he would be able to go home and tell his wife his plans. He vowed to himself to keep the news quiet at Esposito's, his favorite drinking hole, but deep down inside he knew that after a couple of rounds he would be telling all the boys about his active involvement with the man known as Kenyatta.

Yes, thought Turner, tonight I'll have martinis. A man in my position has got to learn to relax, to get the pressures of so mammoth a responsibility off his shoulders.

Frank Turner had waited a long time for an opportunity like this. And now that it had arrived, he was pleased with himself and his feeling of importance. It was all perfect except for one thing. If only that nigger detective hadn't been so fuckin' uppity.

But, Turner decided, he would take care of Benson later.

4

IT WAS NOW EIGHT O'CLOCK Sunday morning. Most of the maimed, wounded, and dead from the inner city had been brought in. The hot, windy Saturday night in Los Angeles had been an especially brutal one. Three murders, twenty-six stabbings, and thirty-two serious wounds from gunshot. As usual, County General had been in a state of chaos throughout the entire night. The nurses, orderlies, interns, and doctors were about exhausted as the bright, clear morning broke over Los Angeles.

For Joe Collins, the night had been especially tiring. The excitement of speaking with Kenyatta, the presence of Elliot Stone, and the constant watch that

the young black orderly attempted to maintain over
the wounded O.E.O. worker.

After his conversation with Kenyatta, Collins had
used every excuse his excited mind could create to
get down to the operating room and check on the
progress of Stone. The surgeon had taken five hours
to extract the shotgun pellets and another hour to
remove the burnt skin and then graft fresh skin from
other parts of Stone's body onto the scorched area.
According to the nurses, Stone was in satisfactory
condition and was expected to live.

Each time Collins returned to the operating room,
he was greeted with a new entourage of policemen
and plainclothes detectives. It was obvious to everyone that Stone was a special patient whom the police
had a very keen interest in. The policy of the hospital with people like Stone was to keep the authorities
as far away as possible from the wounded victim.
More than once, an energetic cop in his desire to
extract information would go to brutal lengths, often-
times resulting in the patient's death. An investigation
had been launched three years before by the NAACP
and their findings had prompted a standing "hands-
off" policy toward patients in County General. The
police would have to wait until the doctor specifical-
ly gave them the go-ahead.

Kenyatta had explained this situation to Collins in
their second phone conversation. He had told the
young orderly that the only time available to them
would be immediately after the operation, when Stone
was to be removed to his bedroom. Otherwise a guard

would be posted, making kidnapping risky to the point of suicide.

Collins told Kenyatta that he understood, and that he would get a nurse to help him remove Stone from the hospital. The fact that Collins had recruited a nurse seemed to impress Kenyatta.

Everything was set. An ambulance with two of Kenyatta's men as attendants would be waiting in the garage beneath the hospital. All that was needed was for Collins to get the man down to the garage. Of course, Collins would have to sacrifice his job at the hospital, but Kenyatta had eased the young man's worries by telling him that he would be well taken care of.

At twenty minutes past eight, Nurse Ellie Jenkins walked quickly out of the operating room and found Joe Collins leaning against the water fountain smoking a cigarette.

"Hey, Joe, you can talk to your friend. They're bringing him out now."

"You goin' take the stretcher, Ellie?" Joe asked excitedly.

"Sure. I got to go now."

The young black nurse turned her back and skipped back into the room. Collins felt inside his white smock and held the snub-nosed .38 lightly. He and Ellie would wheel Stone back into the elevator, along with one other orderly. No one except Joe Collins knew what was to happen after they got inside.

Collins waited next to the door. Ellie and another black orderly pushed open the swinging doors and pushed Elliot Stone toward the elevator. A plasma bottle hung from a rack above his bed. Stone's face was an odd mixture of black and gray. His eyes were closed, but he was breathing.

"How is he?" Collins asked, staring down at the chiseled, handsome face.

"Pretty fine, the doctors say," Ellie answered cheerfully. "Couple of weeks and he'll be normal...."

The elevator doors opened and Ellie and the orderly pushed the stretcher inside the cubicle. Behind him, Collins could hear the approaching footsteps of the police officers. They had been at the coffee machine when Stone had been taken out of the room.

"Could I ride up with you, Ellie?" Collins asked, his hand inside his smock where the .38 rested.

"Sure, Joe," Ellie replied, then turned to the other orderly. "He's a friend," she said.

The elevator doors began to close, but one of the police officers, a huge white man with a large belly, jammed his hand between them and caused the automatic opening device to function.

"I'll ride with you," the officer said in a low, gruff voice.

"'Fraid not, sir," Collins replied. "We're takin' him to the eighth floor. You meet us there."

The cop stared at Collins hard. Obviously the little black nigger would not move. The officer thought for a moment that he would be able to break through hospital policy, but it was apparent that Collins knew the rules. "Okay, eighth floor," the officer said angrily.

Inside the elevator, Collins waited for the doors to

close before he pushed the button for the basement.

"What you doin', Joe?" Ellie asked.

The orderly stood across from Collins. He was a large black man, slow and ponderous, but huge. Collins could feel the man's eyes on him, could feel him beginning to move in his direction. Without bothering to answer Ellie, Collins pulled the pistol from inside his smock.

"Now listen, both of you," he began quickly. "I don't want no kind of jive. Dig? Just stay cool and everything'll be all right!"

The look on Ellie's face was one of shock and horror. She had known Joe Collins for a long time and yet had never seen him like this.

They rode in silence down the three floors to the basement. Finally, the elevator came to a crunching halt. The doors opened and revealed the huge, concrete garage. An ambulance was waiting off to the right, just where Kenyatta said it would be.

"Okay now," Collins said, "let's move him outta here!"

He held the gun on the orderly as the larger man pushed the stretcher out into the garage. Ellie waited until the elevator was empty, then moved out herself.

The two black men driving the ambulance jumped out of the front seat, ran behind, and opened the large swinging doors. They lifted the stretcher up and eased it inside. One of the men was Rufus. He looked at Collins carefully. "You Collins?"

"Yeah," Collins replied.

"Very cool," Rufus said in a way of a compliment.

"You better get yourself in the back. We got some kind of travelin' to do."

Collins turned to Ellie. "Sorry, babe," he began, "but this was heavy shit. You both get out of here, dig?"

Ellie stared at Collins, still not fully comprehending what was happening. The orderly stood next to her, staring with a baleful frown at Collins as he leaped into the rear of the ambulance.

As Collins was about to pull the back door of the ambulance shut, the orderly made his move. Spinning on one heel, the large black man tried to reach the alarm button next to the elevator. Quickly Collins raised his gun, aimed at the man's legs, and fired.

The explosion rang out through the garage, the sound of the gunshot bouncing madly off the pillars and walls. Ellie screamed loudly when she saw the left side of the orderly's leg ripped away by the bullet. She had seen many a victim of shootings, yet had never witnessed a man getting hit by a bullet.

Collins slammed the door to the ambulance, and Rufus made the vehicle squeal loudly as he tore toward the exit.

At the exit gates stood two armed security guards who had seen the shooting at the far end of the garage. They both held .45s, aiming directly at the fast approaching ambulance. Rufus lowered himself behind the wheel and slammed down hard on the accelerator. The two guards began shooting.

Two bullets shattered the windshield of the ambulance. Before either guard had a chance to get in another round, the speeding red vehicle was on top of them. The guard on the passenger side leaped for his life, rolling around on the concrete and finally slamming up against the wall.

The other guard was a little slower than his partner and paid for it with his life. The front of the ambulance smashed into his upper legs and mid-section with a sickening crunch. The white man doubled up, rested for a moment on the hood, then flew off to the side crazily.

His body flew twenty feet through the air like a rag doll before smashing up against a pillar. The guard was wrapped around the post, almost as though he had been stuck there with glue. Then, slowly, he began sliding downward toward the floor. When he hit bottom, his body twisted into a gruesome distortion of what it once had been.

His arms were thrown out of their sockets, twisted completely behind his back. One leg was resting against his side at an upward angle, having been torn completely from its socket. The man's face was smashed into a raw mass of pulp, hair, and flesh. His head was crushed so badly it was now half the size it once had been.

Joe Collins peered out the back window of the ambulance in time to see the man crumpled on the floor. A wave of extreme nausea hit him hard.

Rufus drove like a madman through the empty Sunday morning streets of Los Angeles. He knew it would take at least five minutes, maybe more, before the hospital was aware of what had happened. The only witnesses left alive were the girl and the black orderly.

Kenyatta, Betty, the two nurses, and three of Kenyatta's men were waiting in the alleyway behind Kenyatta's apartment. Rufus pulled the ambulance into the small street and stopped. Joe Collins popped open the rear doors and jumped out. He stood face to face with Kenyatta. The leader towered over the man.

"Collins, my man," Kenyatta said quietly, "I want to thank you for this."

The two black men shook hands while Stone's body was pulled from the ambulance. Within a minute the three Kenyatta men were lugging the stretcher up the stairs and toward Kenyatta's apartment. Rufus climbed back into the ambulance and drove off, with one of Kenyatta's men following him in an old Ford. The entire exchange had taken less than two minutes. Kenyatta had surveyed the windows surrounding the alley, seeing if anyone had looked out to see what was happening. As far as he could tell, no one had.

What once had been the living room in Kenyatta's apartment was now a hospital room, complete with hospital bed, transfusion equipment, and medicines. Waiting inside for the delivery of his patient was a small, heavyset black man, who wore strong glasses and spoke in a soft, orderly voice. When Stone was brought into the room by the two nurses, Dr. Lucius Davis immediately set to work examining the wounded man.

Kenyatta stood next to the door and watched the

small doctor as he pulled Stone's gown up to his neck and began checking the wounds. The young black's body was riddled with small incisions and stitches. His legs were gnarled and covered with grafted pieces of skin. "How does he look?" Kenyatta asked anxiously as Davis replaced Stone's gown.

"Not too bad, Kenyatta. If I had the X rays I could tell you whether or not they got all the metal out. But as far as I can see, they did."

When do you think he'll come around?"

"Well," Davis began, "he's still under the anesthetic. Soon as that wears off, he'll be in a lot of pain. Maybe too much to keep him awake. Might have to give him something."

Kenyatta felt a twinge inside him. He wanted to question Stone, to get an identification of the men who had hit the house. But more than that, he wanted to know what was in the photographs that Stone had taken to the house before the attack. If Stone regained consciousness, then he would try to extract those answers. "Lemme know when he comes around," Kenyatta said, "and I want you and the two nurses here to stand by him every minute. Okay?"

Inside the living room, Kenyatta's small band of close friends sat on the sofa and the chairs. Collins stood against the wall smoking a cigarette. He was still not used to the fact that he was this close to the big man. Everything to him was exciting, a complete change in his life that he had been anticipating for some time.

"As soon as Rufus and Edgar get back," Kenyatta

said to the group, "we'll have it wrapped. Everyone
here did their gigs well. Especially Joe Collins." Then
Kenyatta proceeded to introduce young Collins to
everyone in the room.

"What'll we do now?" Alan, one of Kenyatta's closest men, asked after the introductions.

"We wait," Kenyatta replied. "We wait till Elliot is
well enough. Then we find out who's involved, and
we go from there. Those dudes who brought this shit
down are goin' to pay. They're goin' to pay with their
fuckin' lives!"

No one in the room doubted Kenyatta's words.
They had all heard them before, except for Collins.
And even for the young black man who had just
entered the domain of Kenyatta, the words sent a chill
down his spine. No way in the world would he trade
places with the men responsible for what had happened at the O.E.O. office. Kenyatta's words were not
a warning, nor were they a threat. Simply put, they
were a promise.

Within the hour, Rufus and Edgar returned. The
ambulance had been hidden inside the small warehouse. No one had seen them, and the entire operation had come off without a hitch. The small group
of black men sat down to a large breakfast prepared
by Betty and began discussing their plans for the
future. By the time they had finished breakfast, a general plan was formulated. Collins sat back in his chair
drinking coffee and watching Kenyatta and his men
as they conversed. It was not difficult to believe that

this small group of well-trained black men would bring havoc upon the men responsible.

It was not difficult to believe that, because of what had happened, many men somewhere in Los Angeles would be dead before the week was out.

5

THE FLIGHT FROM DETROIT had given Benson and Ryan time to discuss the case, and both men's reactions to what had gone down inside Turner's office. Most of the conversation had revolved around Benson's reactions to the reappearance of Kenyatta and the conflicting emotions that the black leader stirred inside the black detective. Ryan had tried to calm his partner, insisting that both men were professionals and needed to act accordingly. Deep-seated feelings regarding race, Ryan felt, should never enter the picture.

Benson had argued the point, but deep down inside, the black detective knew that his points were irrelevant. After all, he was still a cop, and once again it came down to the question of turning in his badge or remaining within the structure.

So, as the 747 touched down at Los Angeles International Airport, Detective Benson was resolved within himself to crack the Kenyatta case. He would pursue the matter to its fullest and not compromise because he happened to be a black man. Ryan had accepted his partner's pledge with a troubled smile. He knew Benson too well to believe that the man would be able to turn off all emotions and insight.

Lieutenant Julius Stein of the Los Angeles Police Department was waiting at the passenger terminal when Benson and Ryan emerged from the plane. The tall, bald police officer wore a gray flannel suit and an expression of extreme worry.

"Benson, Ryan?" Stein said when he greeted the partners. "I'm Julius Stein, call me Jules. Welcome to L.A."

The three men shook hands. Stein's eyes flicked back and forth between the white cop and the black cop. He hadn't expected a Negro police officer, and the sight of Benson had obviously caused him some shock.

"We'd like to get to the hospital as fast as possible," Benson began as they walked down the long, white tunnel toward the parking lot.

"Yeah. We've got to get something out of Stone," Ryan added.

Stein shrugged. His suit fit poorly, and the wrinkles in the back and shoulders were accentuated every time he moved. "Well, gentlemen," Stein began hoarsely, "the thing is that little Elliot Stone is no longer with us."

"Fuck! He's dead?" Ryan exclaimed, suddenly seeing all their hopes disappearing in a swift moment.

"No, no," Stein replied quickly. "He's just gone. Vanished! They nabbed him out of County General about two hours ago."

Benson watched the tall, surly lieutenant carefully. His instincts warned him that Stein was not quite as simple and easygoing as he liked people to believe. "Jules," Benson began softly, "you mean some dudes just marched into the goddamn hospital and took him out? Where the hell were the guards?"

Stein shrugged, again throwing out his hands in a gesture of helplessness. "Benson, the damn nig..., uh, excuse me, just a figure of speech..., they had inside people. Someone inside the hospital, namely a black orderly named Joseph Collins."

As they moved out of the main terminal building and into the bright Los Angeles sky, Stein continued his explanation of what had happened at the hospital. He shrugged and moaned and ran his hand across his bald pate for emphasis. Ryan looked at Benson as the man talked. It was either Stein's mannerism or his seemingly casual attitude about the kidnapping of Elliot Stone that worried the two Detroit cops. Maybe, thought Benson, things were different on the West Coast.

It was only the second time in L.A. for Benson and Ryan. The expansiveness of the city was overwhelm-

ing to both detectives. Stein took the San Diego
Freeway up to the Santa Monica, then followed that
across the huge basin and into central Los Angeles.
Benson and Ryan rode in silence until they reached
the city center, with its massive steel and glass tow-
ers resting easily in a vision that just as easily could
have come out of a science fiction book as well as an
architect's drawings.

"How do you guys keep it patrolled, for Christ's
sake?" Benson asked as they turned off the freeway
and headed through the main street toward County
General.

"Helicopters, mobile units..., the whole bit," Stein
explained. "This is a city on wheels, Benson. Cars,
cars, and more cars. It's so fuckin' spread out that
patrol units just don't do the job."

"How many choppers do you guys have?" Ryan
asked.

"Right now, only twelve. Pennies, they always want
to save pennies." Stein shrugged again. Benson was
growing irritated with the man's gestures.

"Listen," Benson began, his rising impatience
showing in his voice, "let's get this over to County.
We can discuss the department later."

"Okay, okay! Just relax! No need to get...how do
you guys say it...uptight?"

Benson chuckled. "Yeah, uptight. That's how we
guys say it."

The scene at County General was chaotic. The
garage was filled with uniformed police, detectives,
and two FBI men who had been brought in on the

case. They explained their presence to Lieutenant Stein on the grounds that, since Stone had been an official of the United States government working in the O.E.O. office, he was under jurisdiction of the Federal Bureau. Benson watched the confrontation between Stein and the Fed and thought he detected an inordinate amount of discomfort in the burly detective. He started to mention his viewpoint to Ryan but felt that it would be better discussed at a later time.

"Can you believe this crap?" Stein complained when he joined Benson and Ryan. "The Feds already. Next thing you know, they'll be wanting the CIA and the goddamn president!"

"Well," Benson said calmly, "it was a federal matter with Stone. I mean, the cat was an employee."

"Yeah, sure, Benson," Stein replied, "but it was just some gang action. We see it all the time down there. Young hoods playing like they're the big time. Too many Mafia movies, that's all."

Once again, Stein's attitude bothered Benson. The man was like a shopper wandering through a men's store, making comments about the quality of fabric and cut of a suit. A multitude of people had already died because of the action Saturday night, and if Benson knew this man, more people were yet to die. Still, this detective whose territory this was treated the matter as if it were an upset stomach. It didn't make sense, but Benson was willing to let it go, call it a fault of the man's character, and pay no more attention to it.

The police photographers were finishing their picture-taking of the garage, and the detectives were completing their interviews with the nurse and the large black orderly. The name "Joseph Collins" had been verified by everyone as the man responsible for the kidnapping. Even the officer on the operating-room floor was able to identify Collins as the man who barred him from riding with the patient to the eighth floor.

After one hour of combing the hospital, retracing the route that Collins had taken with Stone, Benson and Ryan wound up in the cafeteria. Nothing new had been learned and the case was as empty of leads as it had been when the two detectives were flying thirty thousand feet over the Rocky Mountains.

"Well," Benson began, stirring his coffee thoughtfully, "we got ourselves a kidnapped witness, a missing orderly, and not much else."

Ryan laughed. "Except for a detective who looks like he never got over the lost weekend."

"You dug it, too?" Benson asked.

"Yeah. The guy plays a strange game, shuffling around like that as if he were a dog without senses."

Both men stopped short as Stein approached the table. His turned-down mouth was etched into a frown, his eyes glazed from exhaustion. "C'mon," he said loudly, "we got a car ready."

"The O.E.O. office?" Benson asked, happy to be moving again. The lack of sleep was beginning to catch up to him and he felt as if he would collapse if he remained seated doing nothing.

"Yup. The FBI boy'll still be combing it over. But

I thought maybe you guys might want to see it."

Benson and Ryan followed the big detective through the cafeteria and down into the garage. By the time they reached what remained of the small white house, Stein had completed his explanation of what had happened and how they had found Stone. "That the lucky bastard lived was truly amazing," Stein mused.

Benson detected the bitter quality in Stein's voice and reminded himself to discuss it with Ryan again. Either the man was racist, Benson felt, or else he was completely without feeling for his job. In either case, the two detectives should be aware of Stein as an obstacle, someone who would be of no particular help to them.

"Well," Stein said glumly, "there it is."

The small white house that had formerly been head-quarters of the South Central O.E.O. looked as though a bomb had dropped directly into its center. Only the four corner beams remained standing, as well as a slight expanse of charred concrete wall. On that wall was written the name "Black Maria." Other than that, not much was left. Even what once were metal filing cabinets and desks had been melted down into grotesque, twisted shapes.

"Not much here," Ryan said as they approached the house.

"Told you," Stein replied. "Those gangs play rough."

Two uniformed policemen stood guard near the front of the burnt house, while behind them four men wearing khakis and boots sifted through the ashes.

Stein gestured toward the men and explained that they
were Federal agents assigned to the investigation.

Benson and Ryan waited for Stein to direct them
to the Federal men, but instead Stein just stood on the
sidewalk, pulled out a cigar, and lit it. Benson looked
toward Ryan, then back at Stein.

"We'd like to talk to the Federal agents," Benson
said directly.

"Oh, sure, if you think it'll help."

"Can't hurt, Stein," Benson replied, his voice dropping into a familiar cold pattern.

Stein glanced at the tall black detective coldly. His
watery blue eyes were almost void of any feeling.
They seemed, instead, to reflect what was around him.
Benson had been trying for hours to see the man, but
realized that Stein was not to be seen...by anyone.

Three of the Federal men were white and one was
black. Stein walked directly up to the black agent and
spoke with him for a moment, gesturing back at
Benson and Ryan. The agent nodded, then put down
his sifting pan and notepad and walked carefully
across the ashes to where Ryan and Benson waited.

"I'm Agent Comstock," the black man said, holding out his hand to Benson.

"Detective Benson, and my partner Ryan."
Comstock shook Ryan's hand quickly, then turned
back to Benson.

"Well, you boys all the way out from Detroit?"
Comstock said.

"Yes. We feel there may be a tie-in here to a man
named Kenyatta."

"Ah, yes," Comstock said. "The famed Detroit massacre. We were in on the thing after the Vegas crash, but no one knew where the dude went. Can you believe that?"

Ryan spoke up for the first time. "We've been dealing with Kenyatta for a long time. Nothing that fucker does surprises us anymore."

Comstock laughed and was joined by Stein. Benson stared at the Federal agent, noticing for the first time how light the man's skin was. The usual heavy features of the black man were absent. Instead, Comstock displayed a soft, almost feminine countenance.

Ryan noticed the troubled look on his partner's face and spoke again, this time loud enough to stop what he felt was false laughter. "What have you guys found?"

Comstock turned to Ryan, his smile evaporating. "Nothin' much. This is routine, the usual shit. Get a place like this goin' in the ghetto and you're bound to get yourself burned to the ground sooner or later. Couple blacks get turned down for aid..., anything'll do it."

Benson could see that nothing was going to come of this visit with Comstock. The man was cynical and almost "white" in his whole attitude. "Okay, brother," Benson said, emphasizing the friendly greeting. "If you do happen on something, you can reach us through Stein's office at headquarters."

"Yeah, fine. But I doubt it." Comstock nodded to Benson and Ryan, then turned and started to move back toward the house. Benson noticed that the

Federal man did not nod to Stein.

"Okay, you boys look like a little sleep would do you some good. I'll drive you to your hotel." Stein seemed jovial as he slid in behind the steering wheel and started up the car. "How long you guys plan to spend out here?" he asked as he pulled onto Compton Boulevard and headed back toward the central city.

"All depends, Stein," Benson replied. "All depends."

The worried look that Stein gave Benson did not escape the black man's eyes. Instead, it served to fuel something inside Benson that was beginning to plague him.

Stein had gotten Benson and Ryan a room at the Biltmore Hotel in downtown Los Angeles. The old hotel located across from Pershing Square was an anachronism of what once was downtown Los Angeles. Its plush carpeting and elegant chandeliers had deteriorated with age. And old men, tired of the darkness of the streets, inhabited the lobby.

"Well, gentlemen," Stein said as he prepared to leave the two detectives, "it's not much. But with prices today...." Stein shrugged and closed the door behind him.

Benson sat down on the bed and lit a cigarette. Already the exhaustion was overtaking him. It was now twelve noon in Los Angeles. Taking the time difference into consideration, both men had been up for twenty-four hours. "Man, I don't know why the fuck we came out here," Benson said disgustedly.

Ryan looked at his partner and knew that the man was suffering from the same feelings of helplessness that he felt himself. What had been a solid lead had suddenly disappeared, and the two men were stuck with what seemed like an idiot of a police detective to work with.

"You know why, Ryan?" Benson asked after a long silence. "'Cause some fuckin' little asshole captain back in Detroit wants a promotion, that's why!"

"Yeah, okay. Turner sees us as a feather in his cap if he gets Kenyatta. But we didn't know that Stone would slip out of the hands of the guys here."

"Yeah," Benson said. "That's another thing that bothers me. Fuckin' dude just gets moved out of there. Man, that's pretty damned inept when they can't hold a man—especially a man who was in the condition Stone was in!"

"I know, I know," Ryan agreed, stripping down to his shorts and flopping onto the bed. "This whole thing stinks. No one seems to know what's going on or, for that matter, even cares."

"I'll tell you something, Ryan. We got to get ourselves on the streets. We're goin' nowhere fast with this schmuck Stein. He's either an idiot or a fuckin' plant. Hard for me to believe he's a cop."

Suddenly, Ryan sat upright and looked at his partner. "Listen, Ben, remember that guy in Detroit named Johnny? Johnny Miller! Out on parole. A real junkie?"

"Yeah, sure, I remember him."

"Okay, the dope on him was that he sang for Detroit cops. He played a two-way street until it got too crowded, and then he left. I was told by Jack in Vice that if I ever needed anything in L.A. to get in touch with him. Supposedly the guy's always where the action is."

Benson forgot his exhaustion. Ryan had made a worthwhile suggestion. Working together, with men on the streets—junkies, pimps, and winos—had always brought faster results to the detectives. For some reason, as soon as either of them stepped inside a city hall or an official building, they ran into roadblocks. Street people were always easier.

"What do you say, Ben?" Ryan asked.

"Yeah. Get your tail into gear and let's talk to this dude. I mean, if there's some Kenyatta action goin' down in this town, the cat'll know—not to mention gang violence!" Benson laughed bitterly.

Ryan was on the phone in a second, talking to the man named Jack who worked the Vice detail in the motor city. With satisfaction, Benson watched as his partner wrote down Johnny Miller's street address and telephone number.

"We got him!" Ryan said happily as he slammed down the phone. "Two o'clock this afternoon on the pier at Santa Monica!"

"The dude's really willin', isn't he?"

"Yup. Been makin' it all his life singing songs for the cops. No reason for him to stop now." Ryan lit a cigarette and was just about to relax on the bed when the telephone rang. He picked it up, listened for a moment, then said, "Okay. Be right down." Ryan turned to Benson. "That was Stein. They've just arrested the leader of the Black Maria."

Benson eyed his partner for a moment, then slowly reached over to the table and drew out a cigarette. It was the last one, and Benson crumpled the empty pack slowly, then tossed a perfect shot into the wastebasket. "You ever get the feelin', partner, that we're on a downhill train without brakes?" he said very slowly.

Ryan began dressing. "No brakes, Ben," Ryan replied, "but a whole lot of power!"

Benson stared straight ahead and smirked. Suddenly he bolted off the bed, getting to his feet in one swift motion. "Well," he began in mock enthusiasm, "let's go see Stein and his man, shut the case down, and get back on that plane this afternoon. I'd imagine the dude already has tickets for us, being thoughtful as he is!"

Both men laughed as they dressed. But underneath was the very real suspicion that they were being railroaded.

Lucius Davis sat alone in the small interrogation room inside the Los Angeles police headquarters. The eighteen-year-old black man smoked a cigarette, staring sullenly at the table in front of him. With his huge Afro, his tall, lanky frame, and the cold, distant look in his eye, he gave the impression of a snake, coiled and ready to strike at any time.

"There's the…uh, suspect," Stein said proudly as he and the two detectives from Detroit stood behind the one-way mirror looking in on Davis. "We took the bastard's jacket, the one with the Maria seal. You can see that later."

Benson nodded. "Can we talk to him?" he asked.

"Sure! Sure!" Stein bubbled. "No problem! It's not every day we get such an open-and-shut case, Benson. No. This is one of the better scenes of my lifetime!"

Stein led Benson and Ryan into the room. The all-white, low-ceilinged cubicle, with its acoustical tile and low-hanging fluorescent lights, was entirely different from the interrogation rooms back in Detroit. It was modern and clean, no cigarette burns on the floor or table, no rotting woodwork, and no smell of decay. Yet, in its own distinctive way, the room was just as oppressive and confining.

"Gentlemen," Stein began when they entered the room, "Lucius Davis, president of the gang known as the Black Maria."

The tall black youth looked quickly to Ryan, then to Benson. Beneath the shock of hair the black's eyes were cold and hard. Yet they seemed to soften when he saw Benson's. Both men were black, and both knew that, no matter what anybody said, they were set apart, distinctive if only by the color of their skin.

"Well," Benson began, "you got yourself a heavy rap, Davis."

Davis continued to look directly at Benson. "I'm innocent, man. Innocent!" he said softly.

"Yeah, yeah," Stein interjected loudly. "Innocent! You know what we found on him? Smack, gentlemen! A packet of smack and a kit! Innocent my ass!"

The smack was something new. Stein hadn't mentioned it before, and the sudden presence of this element surprised Benson. "Heroin, eh?" he began, now looking down at Davis. "You shoot?" he asked.

Davis shrugged. "No, man, we don't shoot no stuff. We're all clean."

"How many times you hear that pitch?" Stein interrupted loudly.

This time Benson had had enough of the lieutenant's interruptions and brash comments. He turned and faced the large, paunchy man and stared at him coldly. "Listen, Stein," Benson began in a voice that rattled the white acoustical tiles, "would you mind just shutting up for one goddamn minute? Ever since we got here you been shooting off your asinine mouth, telling me and my partner what we ought to think and what we ought not to think! Man, we didn't come out here just to listen to someone like you!"

Stein turned red. His breathing grew heavy, and his eyes seemed to water. He took a small step backward, then tried to smile. "Sorry," he began very softly, "but I've seen it before. All of it. I just thought...."

"I know what you just thought," Benson interrupted, "but that's not the way we work. Maybe out here you guys take everything for granted, but in Detroit we got some real bad problems, some real bad conditions, and we can't take anything for granted!"

Benson finished and turned back to Davis. The young black quickly lowered his eyes, but Benson knew that he had been watching him closely. He hoped that he had done two things—put Stein into a defensive position and instilled some amount of trust in Davis.

The game, as it was known in police departments throughout the country, was played often. It involved two officers staging a phony verbal fight between themselves, getting the prisoner to open up as one officer took his side. Normally, the game was set up, contrived, but this time Benson had meant every word. Ryan knew that his partner was for real, that he wasn't playing with Stein. But the lieutenant, who was now standing against the far wall, began to think he knew what Benson was after. The redness disappeared from his sagging jowls and he broke out into a semi-grin.

"Okay, Detective, have it your fuckin' way," Stein said, winking at Ryan. Ryan did all he could to keep his fists at his side. Either Stein was the biggest idiot he had ever seen or else he was an asshole. Ryan knew when his partner was really angry, and any man in his right mind would have been able to tell, also. He couldn't believe that Stein was unable to distinguish the real from the phony. Yes, Ryan thought heatedly, the man is a supreme idiot!

Benson glanced up at his partner. He could tell what Ryan was thinking. He turned away and took a seat opposite Davis. "Listen, Davis," Benson began quietly, "would you mind rolling up your sleeves?"

Davis looked at the black detective, and for the first time his eyes softened. He nodded, then quickly unbuttoned his cuffs and pulled the sleeves up around his biceps. Benson reached across the table and took the young black's wrist, examining his right arm first, then repeating the process with the left arm.

"Okay, Davis, pull 'em down." Slowly, Benson got

to his feet. "Funny," he began, looking at Ryan first, then at Stein, "you accuse this man of using heroin, yet there's no track marks on his arms, no puncture holes. No signs at all."

"We found heroin in his apartment, Benson," Stein said coldly.

"You give this man a physical?" Ryan asked.

"Of course not!" Stein protested.

"I see," Benson said. He looked down at the black youth. The man was healthy looking, his eyes were clear and strong. There were no signs of the drug in him at all. No redness around the eyes, no paleness in the skin. His breathing and his pulse, which Benson had checked while examining Davis' arms, were both normal. No signs at all of a user. What there were signs of, however, was a plant.

"What other evidence do we have on Davis?" Benson asked Stein.

"Nothing except the obvious. The bastard is the president of the Black Maria. And the Black Maria burned down an office of the federal government. The FBI is satisfied, so why the questions?"

Benson frowned, pulled out a fresh pack of cigarettes, and offered one to Davis. The black youth accepted and inhaled deeply after Benson lit it. "No reason," the black detective began. "Just asking, Stein, just asking."

Stein smiled, then hitched up his pants and knocked on the door twice. A uniformed officer opened it and stood aside to let the men out. "Well," Stein said, "if you gentlemen are finished…. Arraignment is tomorrow for our friend here, so maybe then you can consider the case open and closed."

Benson started to leave the room, and the man who had been arrested on charges of murder, arson, and possession of heroin watched him closely. Before closing the door behind him, Benson turned and looked back at the black youth. "Don't blow it, man. We'll be back."

Lucius Davis nodded gravely. It appeared at that moment that Ed Benson, a black cop working alien territory, was all the hope he had.

The pier at Santa Monica was crowded. Young couples, mostly blacks and Chicanos, strolled the decaying structure, stopping at the arcade to play the pinball machines and games of chance. The old merry-go-round spun with a cacophony of sound as the ancient calliope belted out its eerie, almost nightmarish music. The day was cool, much cooler than it should have been for this time of year. And a low bank of fog sat only yards off the coast.

Detectives Benson and Ryan stood at the end of the pier watching old men and young boys lined up along the railing holding their fishing rods suspended over the side. Ryan kept turning back and searching out the expanse of pier, looking for the man from Detroit. Finally he spotted the small, slim figure of Johnny Miller ambling casually toward them as though he were a tourist taking in the sights.

"There he is," Ryan said. "Shit, he's really gotten thin."

Benson turned and glanced at the little dude. Miller was dressed with the haughty air of a black pimp—small continental hat pushed back, tight-fitting shark-skin pants, open velour shirt, and a tight-fitting plaid jacket. He approached the two detectives slowly, taking one last look behind him before committing himself to the corner of the pier where Benson and Ryan waited.

"Hey, my man," Miller said in a staccato, strained voice, "what's happenin'?"

The thin black man, his eyes bulging like a lizard's, constantly watching and waiting for his prey, gripped Ryan's hand with the full clasp, then turned to Benson and performed the three-way, thumb-hook-to-finger-tip to full grasp handshake. Benson performed the shake well and noticed how tight the unnatural Miller seemed to carry it out.

"You dudes a long, long way from home," Miller stated, leaning against the railing and inserting a cigarette into a gold-plated holder. "Shit, this ain't no Detroit, dig?"

Ryan laughed. "Yeah, you didn't have a gold-plated holder in Detroit."

Miller grunted a low-keyed moan. "Fuck no, Ryan. Action out here's pretty groovy, if you dig where I'm comin' from. Real casual-like and hip. Not too much jive."

Benson watched Miller, thinking how he had seen so many guys like him before. Blacks without the brawn or the brain to really make it in the underworld. But dudes who considered themselves too hip to go straight, marry, and raise children. With no place to go, they made their living using their ears and their eyes. Listening to the action on the streets, making some bread off the cops or off the gang lords, depending on who wanted the information and how much they were willing to pay. Sometimes they would even deal a little shit just to keep themselves rolling in the white powder. But the real name of their game was "singing," playing the world's oldest tune for a price.

"So what's happenin'?" Miller asked after inquiring about the situation in Detroit.

Ryan cleared his throat, then turned to lean against the rail and stare out to the ocean. "What do you know about the Black Maria?" he asked.

Miller shrugged his shoulder, took a long drag, and looked at Ryan. "I know lot of shit, man. But then again, I'm into a special gig with my information, you dig it? I mean, man's got to live, and I kind of dig my style."

Benson pulled out a twenty-dollar bill from his jacket pocket and handed it to Miller. Miller slipped the bill into his pants pocket and leaned back against the rail.

"Well," he began slowly, "the Black Maria. Shit, what could you dudes want with a bunch of cats like them?"

"Just answer the questions, Miller," Benson stated.

"All right, man, no need to get uptight. Okay, they're small-time, dig? Work out of Compton and Manchester area. Like, most of the dudes are high school or just out, know what I mean? From what I hear, they got a philosophy. You know, niggers like havin' them philosophies these days."

"What kind of philosophies?" Benson asked quickly.

"Well, you know, clean shit. The straight-ahead thing. No dope, no crime, black is beautiful, and all that crap."

Benson and Ryan exchanged glances. This was not what they had expected. Although Benson had had a hint of it down at the police station, it was still a surprise to hear the facts from Miller. "Go on, my man," Benson urged, now beginning to feel an affinity for the little black dude, not because of the man himself, but because of what the man was telling him.

"Well, that's about all the shit. They just a bunch of phony toughs, dig, who like to come down heavy on us dudes out in the streets. That's 'bout it, my man." Miller looked from Benson to Ryan, then down at the ground. Obviously there was still something left inside of him that detested telling the authorities everything he knew.

"You ever hear of a man named Kenyatta?" Benson asked after a silence. He watched Miller's face closely, trying to pick up some clue to the man's reaction.

"Kenyatta? Shit, man, everyone's heard of him."

"No," Benson said, "not in Detroit. Out here. I mean, in Watts. Anything comin' down the tube about him?"

Miller pulled the cigarette holder from between his lips. The name Kenyatta had kindled responses in every black man who had ever had anything to do with Detroit. Either he was a feared and hated black man or he was a savior. "Shit!" Miller exclaimed, almost whistling the words out, "you layin' down a trip or somethin'? You standin' there tellin' me you think the dude is in L.A.?"

"We're not sure, Miller," Ryan said, pulling out a hundred-dollar bill and placing it in Miller's breast pocket. "But we want you to start asking questions. An O.E.O. office was hit last night, supposedly by the Maria gang. Two of the men inside were former Kenyatta men from Detroit. We think there's a connection someplace. You know what Kenyatta's thoughts were about dope, so we think maybe the cats who hit him were the big runners here. You see?"

Benson watched the small man's reactions. Miller was not used to the big time, and Kenyatta, no matter where the man went, was always involved in the high-stakes players. It shook the little dude to even be talking about it.

"Well," Benson asked, "will you do it? There'll be plenty of bread comin' down the pipe. If you dig?"

Miller looked from Benson to Ryan. His large eyes were a little bigger now, and his cool, hip manner had disappeared. "You dudes askin' a lot of shit. I just start openin' my mouth an' they'll close it quicker than a fuckin' bear trap! Shit!"

"Listen," Ryan began, trying to soothe Miller. "No need to ask questions or take any chances. Just keep your ears open and see what's happening. Now that you know where the connections are, you might be able to pick up on some shit."

Miller was still shaken. But when Benson slipped him another twenty-dollar bill and said, "I told you, man, there's bread to be made," Miller seemed to relax.

"Okay," the dude said finally. "I'll keep it open and see what's comin' down. Can't promise you nothin', though."

Benson laughed. "Miller," he began, "you got yourself one hell of a rep around police headquarters. Let's see if it's all true, shall we?"

"Some rep. Shit, better I was a fuckin' pimp!"

"Don't know," Benson joked. "Those fuckin' broads can get pretty mean sometimes."

Miller laughed. "You ever seen Kenyatta when that dude got a fire goin'? Man, he's a fuckin' holocaust!"

Miller laughed, but Benson could see that the laughter came from fear. It was always shocking to him how one man, through a reputation, could instill such fear in other men. Kenyatta was one of those men, a legend in his own time.

As Miller walked away from the two detectives, Benson and Ryan watched him. At first, the well-dressed black man had moved stiffly, as though trying to keep a burden from pressuring him into a slouch. But as he moved farther down the pier, he began stroking along, bouncing a little with each step.

"The guy's frightened," Ryan commented when Miller had disappeared into the crowd.

"You told him an awful lot. Maybe too much." Benson had wanted to stop Ryan's discussion of the O.E.O. incident earlier. No one outside the department

knew that the two men inside had been former
Kenyatta men. And now Miller knew.

"No sweat," Ryan said confidently. "The guy walks
a fucking tightrope. He hasn't got friends, and he
hasn't got enemies. He lives on the outside. Nobody'll
listen to him."

"Yeah? Well, we're paying him money to listen to
him. Anyway, let's hope he comes up with something," Benson said.

Ryan nodded. "Yeah, he will. He's got to. We're
being pushed pretty damn hard from the inside on this
one."

"Not just us," Benson replied. "They're going to
fry that kid Davis. And we ain't got much fuckin'
time!"

The determination and the anger was building
inside Benson again, and Ryan knew it. They were
both up against a strange, almost invisible block wall,
trying to break through a maze of half-truths and
bureaucratic jumble. Both detectives' instincts told
them that something was terribly wrong. For Ryan, it
was a professional sense of pride that drove him. But
for Benson, it was something else.

The man was black, and it made a difference.

6

KENYATTA STOOD BEHIND the small bar in his apartment and refilled Edgar's and Rufus' glasses with Jack Daniels. It was the second fifth of whiskey used already. The night was still young, only about ten o'clock. The men, four others besides Rufus and Edgar, had been gathered inside the well-furnished living room for three hours.

In the bedroom, Betty and two nurses, plus the doctor, sat and attended to Elliot Stone. He had been sleeping since being taken out of the hospital. The anesthesia had not yet worn off, and the doctor had been giving him a series of cortisone shots to minimize the pain when the wounded man did come to.

"There you go, my man," Kenyatta said after pouring the shot into Rufus' glass. "Go easy. It's goin' be a long fuckin' night."

"Yeah," Rufus said, taking a slow sip of the whiskey. "We don't know, do we?"

Kenyatta looked at his friend determinedly, almost coldly. "Just a matter of time, my man. When Elliot comes to, then we'll know."

The four men sitting along the couch and on the chairs listened to Kenyatta closely. They were all black men, all dressed in business suits, and all well-trained Kenyatta men. Almost all of the men had shaved heads and none wore mustaches or long sideburns.

There was Duke Simms from the Valley, Amos Cortner from West Los Angeles, "Little" Mike Allen from East Los Angeles, and finally Stonewall Manfred from Compton. Each man, representing over five hundred Kenyatta recruits, had been called into the meeting by the man himself. None of them had been aware of Elliot Stone and his operation at the O.E.O. office. Kenyatta had managed his growing organization with the idea that no one section knew the operation of another. That way, in the case of a massive raid, he would be able to control the leakage of information and insure the survival of the other sectors.

Kenyatta had learned well from the failures of the Black Panthers in the East. He had studied their operation and had learned where they had made their mistakes. Basically, they had been too well organized for their own good. And the government, seeking to destroy their threatening existence, had been able to strike quick and hard at the leaders, thus dismantling the entire operation with a swift, powerful stroke. Kenyatta would not allow that same thing to happen to his people.

Stonewall Manfred leaned forward and stared down at the glass of Jack Daniels he held in his hands. "Listen, Kenyatta," he began in a baritone voice, "we got to find out who hit the fuckin' O.E.O. 'fore we make our move."

Kenyatta listened as Manfred spoke at length about the possibilities of an all-out gang war in the ghettos, a war that would destroy every organized section of blacks in the city. Finally, Manfred finished and sat back.

"You're right, Stonewall," Kenyatta said. "But once we do know where it's comin' from, we got to get it ourselves. We got to move in there and blow the whole fuckin' operation!"

Amos Cortner, considered by all to be the coolest head in the group, listened intently to Kenyatta's words. The man had seen Kenyatta this way before, when emotionalism and rage took over, leaving the man's reasoning powers suppressed by the mighty forces of his hatred and anger. He decided to speak up now, knowing that Kenyatta was still in the throes of his own anger.

"Listen, Kenyatta," Cortner began, "we all dig where you're comin' from. We know it, an' we all feel the same way 'bout those bastards. But we got to keep somethin' else in mind, too."

Kenyatta put his drink down on the bar and leaned forward. He admired Cortner and respected his opinion. "Okay, Amos. I'm listening."

"Well, like Stonewall said, we don' wanna start no fuckin' gang war. Not because we couldn't wipe their motherfuckin' asses but because it wouldn't do us any good. When Stone wakes up and lays it on us, we'll be in a position to do one of two things. We could blow the fuckers off the face of the earth, or we could go inside their organization, find out if it's a street operation or if there's heavier shit goin' down, then make our decision." Cortner waited anxiously for Kenyatta's reply.

Kenyatta glanced around the room. The black faces were watching him intently, waiting for him to give his reply. Finally, the bald-headed leader spoke. "Okay, I can dig where you're at, Cortner. We'll wait till we hear from Stone. No action till then."

Cortner breathed a sigh of relief. Secretly, he had been fearing Kenyatta's temper. The man would just as soon take to the streets and start murdering any man he thought might have had anything to do with the hit at the O.E.O. offices. That, Cortner knew, would have been suicide, and in more ways than one.

Since Kenyatta's arrival on the West Coast, the organization had been built slowly and painstakingly. Barely a handful of men knew of Kenyatta's existence, and most of those men were sitting in the room at that very moment. The element of secrecy was maintained as a safeguard, and also as a means of securing the most information possible.

Every man sitting in that room believed firmly that a huge organization existed outside Watts that supplied the junkies, the high school kids, and the young black girls of that ghetto with heroin. Each man had witnessed, in his own way, the breakdown of life around him as more and more of the white powder flowed into their communities.

And each man had made a commitment to someday get to the root of the operation and destroy it. That goal could not be put into jeopardy by hitting some small-time junkie somewhere who they thought was responsible for two deaths and Stone's injury.

The decision to wait had been made. The men settled themselves down for a long night. Betty made sandwiches and passed them around. The four section leaders played poker. Kenyatta and his two closest men, Rufus and Edgar, stood around the bar drinking Jack Daniels and talking softly amongst themselves.

At ten-thirty that same evening, young Joe Collins was walking along Fifty-third Street toward Compton Avenue. The small, young black man carried a suitcase and a jacket draped across one shoulder. His movements were purposeful, and he walked quickly because he was heading back toward Kenyatta's apartment.

That evening, after Elliot Stone had been secured in the bedroom with the doctor and nurses, Kenyatta had told Collins that he wanted the young man to stay with him in his apartment. "We can't risk having you on the streets," Kenyatta had said, warning Collins not only about the police but also about the same people who had hit Stone's office. Collins had insisted on going back to his mother's small house alone and telling her himself that he would not see her for a couple of days, maybe weeks, and possibly even months.

Hurriedly, Collins had run home. His mother, now into her sixties, sat in the living room watching the television set that Collins had bought for her the previous Christmas. She was an old woman, her body was shriveled and little hope or joy remained in her dark, sagging eyes. Only when she saw her one surviving son did she express a glint, a glimmer of happiness.

Joe Collins had once had two older brothers, but both men had been called up by the Army after the Tet Offensive in the late sixties. They were both killed within a week of each other in front-line action. Collins had read the reports and had heard the rumors saying that black men were virtual guinea pigs in the jungle war. Collins had believed what he had read.

Now he stood in front of his mother, a woman who had lost two sons already, and tried to explain to her why he was leaving. Her eyes were sometimes cold, sometimes blank as her youngest son stammered through his explanation. The old, neat house was dark except for the light of the television, but Collins could see the hurt he was causing inside the old woman.

"I'm sorry, Mom," he said softly, "but it's somethin' I got to do. I'll be back. Don't you worry 'bout that!"

The old woman nodded. She reached out and took

her son's hand and squeezed it. Joe knew at that moment that she understood. "Thank you," he whispered into her ear. The woman nodded again, then took his other hand and placed it on hers. She held him like that for a moment longer, then let him go.

Joe stood up and went into his bedroom and began packing a suitcase. He could hear the inane canned laughter of a television comedy show, then listened as the show broke for a commercial. Two black people, a man and a woman, were glowing idiotically over the merits of a soap detergent. Joe listened for a moment longer and knew that what he was doing was right.

The young black crossed Compton Boulevard near the line of bars and nightclubs. They were fairly quiet on this Sunday evening, and only a few ravaged-looking hookers stood on the sidewalk outside.

Turning the corner and walking down Manchester, Joe Collins found himself on a dark part of the street. He began walking faster. It was at this point that he realized there was a car behind him, pacing him step for step and about sixty feet away.

The young black man's heart began pumping. He heard again in his mind the warning from Kenyatta. But then, he reasoned, possibly it was Kenyatta himself. No, he thought, Kenyatta would have stopped and picked him up. Collins realized at that moment that he was a sitting duck for whoever was in that car. There was nothing to do but try to escape.

A small, dark alley stood about fifty feet ahead of him. Without missing a beat, the young orderly broke into a frantic run toward the alley. The blood was rushing through his brain, and only vaguely did he hear the car accelerate behind him.

His feet slipped on the pavement as he tried to make the right turn into the alleyway without losing a step. Trash cans tumbled about him. He got to his feet again and could see the reflection of the car's headlights on the opposite wall.

The alley was nothing more than a loading driveway for the warehouse at the far end. There, a loading dock stood, its platform six feet off the ground. Behind that was a corrugated metal door. There was no exit from the dark cavern. All the passages were sealed by brick walls and the loading dock itself.

Collins scrambled frantically toward the dock. He knew he was trapped, but the act itself of attempting to escape was the only thing holding it together. His heart beating wildly, he jumped onto the small ledge in front of the metal door.

The car turned into the alley and moved slowly toward where Collins stood. He was blinded by the headlights and could not see how many men were inside. The car stopped ten feet in front of the dock.

Collins was backed up against the metal door. He could feel the ridges digging into his back as he pushed himself with all his strength against the corrugated metal. He prayed that he could somehow melt through that door and regain his life inside the warehouse behind it.

Doors opened on either side of the car, and Collins could hear the movement of men as they got out. He thought he detected the quick, almost imperceptible glint of metal.

"Man," Collins shouted into the blinding head-lights. "I ain't done nothin'…, please!!!"

There was silence from the other side of the lights, the only noise being the purring of the engine.

The young black peered through the glare of lights. In his last moment he was being blinded, unable to see even his own death.

Two explosions rang out in the alleyway. One from either side of the car. The first blast hit Joe Collins in the face, ripping away his nose and right eye. His brain matter was plastered against the metal door behind him. Later that night, the coroner would find his right ear thirty feet away, lying like a piece of garbage in the small alley.

The second blast, within a mini-second of the first, hit him in the stomach. The shells penetrated his flesh from one side to another, tearing his guts out of the safe confines of his body. By the time the two shots had been fired, there was more of the black youth on the metal door than there was on the landing.

In his last moment on earth, Joe Collins had seen two bright flashes as the guns had been fired. He had imagined that he was standing in the jungles of Southeast Asia, and that his two brothers had once been walking where the two land mines had explod-ed. Their bodies had disappeared instantly, and with them Joe Collins had entered the eternal blackness.

At precisely the same moment that Joe Collins was

destroyed by assassins' bullets, Elliot Stone regained consciousness.

The wounded man opened his eyes and saw the small room, the face of the doctor, and the pretty face of Janie, one of Betty's nurses. For a split second, Stone felt a twinge of panic surge through his brain. He knew he wasn't in the hospital, but other than that he had no idea what was happening to him.

Through the cloud of his growing awareness, he heard the doctor yell the name of Kenyatta. Relief flooded through Stone instantly as he realized that he was under the care of the only man he could trust.

When Kenyatta entered the room, he found Elliot Stone smiling. "Hey, my man," Kenyatta said happily.

"Kenyatta?" Stone whispered, "I can't believe this shit, man. What's happenin'?"

Kenyatta grinned and rested his hand on Stone's shoulder. "Man, we got you out of that fuckin' hospital. Couldn't let you hang around there, my man. No way."

"How?" Stone asked.

"We had a man inside, a kid named Joe Collins. He'll be here soon. A good fuckin' man, that kid."

Stone felt himself lighten immediately. It was good to hear Kenyatta speak of his men, especially with the kind of pride and care he used when they had done something well. Obviously, this kid Collins had done well.

"What about the others...in the house?" Stone asked after a brief silence.

Kenyatta shook his head. "Man, those fuckers did

it in. Ain't no way Jimmy or Frank could have made it through."

"Shit," Stone said. The night was coming back to him as he talked with Kenyatta. The nightmare of standing there, knowing the men who held the shotguns were going to pull the trigger. The flash, then the pain, and then the fire. He remembered his fantasy of diving through the Notre Dame line and into the end zone, and chuckled.

"What's so damn funny, Elliot?" Kenyatta asked, grateful to see Stone laughing.

"Jus' thinkin' 'bout what went through my head when I was gettin' out of that fuckin' house. Man, I thought I was playin' football again…, the Notre Dame game."

Kenyatta laughed. "My man, you did 'bout as well as you did in that game. No shit!!!"

The two black men reminisced about the game for a few minutes. Kenyatta had not been there, but Stone had been able to obtain the films. At a party earlier that spring Stone had proudly shown Kenyatta and a number of friends his moment of glory captured on film. The ex-football player was not conceited. The way he explained it was by saying that very few men have a moment like that in their lifetimes, and he was simply damned proud of his.

It was really as simple as that with Stone. He knew the honkies and their motherfuckin' system would try to take everything away from him and his people. But this, that moment on a Saturday afternoon, was something that no one would ever be able to take.

Finally, the conversation turned to the previous night. Kenyatta had asked Stone what he had been carrying in the film when they were hit.

It took a moment before Stone could reconstruct everything in his mind. The film, he remembered that, and the phone call, and then the discussion with Frank and Jimmy. Yes, they had made a link, had discovered something in the operations of the dope ring in Watts. Stone thought hard, and suddenly the picture returned and the pieces fell into place.

"Okay, Kenyatta," Stone said softly. "I've got the shit together."

"Okay, Elliot. Lay it on me, my man."

Kenyatta leaned forward and listened intently. Stone took a deep breach and began speaking.

"We knew about this dude, Wilbur Chamus," Stone began, his voice now without emotion. "What we didn't know was where his junk was comin' from. First off, we knew he had connections downtown with the cops. His street-corner pushers would get busted and be out within like a couple of hours. You dig?"

"Had to be in Narcotics, workin' right with him," Kenyatta mused.

"Yeah, exactly," Stone replied. "Well, we had Chamus, and we knew about his street people. But then we stumbled onto what appeared to be a contact. A white dude, a man I would recognize, would come by Wilbur's place over on Fifty-fifth Street."

"Yeah," Kenyatta added. "The Paris Club?"

"Right. The two dudes would meet like every third Tuesday of the month, the white motherfucker carryin' a briefcase. We had pictures...shit." Stone stopped for a moment, realizing for the first time what the fire had done.

"It's okay, man. No way we can change what's happened."

"Yeah," Stone said, still upset. "Shit, those fuckin' photos would have sealed it." There was a silence for a moment. Both men stared at the floor, and then finally Stone returned to his subject.

"Those pictures, Kenyatta, showed the dude, what he was bringin', and when. We had it all. Especially that white motherfucker who has to be the main contact outside the city. Or at least a lead to the big man."

Kenyatta remained silent. He had heard of Wilbur Chamus but had thought nothing more of him than as a street-corner hustler. Within a week, Stone had unraveled a complex organization that had involved Chamus, a white pusher, and a network of street pushers. There was no doubt now that Chamus was the man they would hit in Watts.

"We're goin' hit Chamus, Elliot," Kenyatta stated coldly.

Stone looked at his man, then frowned. "No, man," he began. "We got bigger fish to fry than that nigger. We got to find out who that whitey is. You dig where I'm comin' from? I mean, all of us know ain't just niggers out there on the streets peddlin' that shit. We know there's some pretty powerful white motherfuckers behind the whole thing. An' now we got ourselves a chance to nail 'em!"

Kenyatta listened to Stone. Basically, he was say-

ing the same thing that Cortner had said earlier that
evening.

"Listen, my man," Stone said, resting his hand on
Kenyatta's arm, "we'll get the bastards in the end. We
can't shoot our wad till then, bro. No way."

Kenyatta knew that Stone was right. He nodded.
"Okay, man, we'll infiltrate. I got a line on some stuff
from Algiers. I'll set up delivery."

Stone smiled. At least now, after all his efforts,
there would still be some kind of a payoff. "You goin'
into the dope business! Man, I never thought I'd see
the fuckin' day!"

Kenyatta laughed along with Stone. Deep down
inside, though, both men knew just how serious the
situation was.

The doctor came into the room and told Kenyatta
that Stone needed rest and to leave the room. The two
men shook hands and agreed to talk again in the morning. Kenyatta watched as the doctor gave Stone his
injection of cortisone.

"See you tomorrow, brother," Kenyatta said as he
left the room.

"Yeah, tomorrow, man!" Stone said sleepily.

When Kenyatta entered the living room he noticed
Rufus standing next to the bar. The man's face was
tight, and his mouth formed a grimace.

"What's happenin', my man?" Kenyatta asked.

Rufus looked at the other men in the room before
speaking. "Joe Collins, Kenyatta."

"Joe? What about Joe?"

"He was hit tonight. 'Bout two blocks from here."

Kenyatta looked at the men in the room. His first impulse was to pull his arms out of the closet, get his men together and hit Wilbur Chamus. But he remembered what he had discussed with Stone, and he knew deep inside that a mere hit wouldn't pay for all the damage that had been done.

They would have to break open the entire organization. And the only way to do that was to get inside. Kenyatta immediately began laying plans to get a pound of uncut heroin into the country. With that amount of white powder and his virtual lack of identity, Kenyatta figured that he would be able to crack any organization, no matter how large.

At that moment, on that windy Saturday night in South Central Los Angeles, no man could have imagined just how large and powerful an organization they were going to infiltrate.

Had they, they probably would have satisfied themselves with the murder of Wilbur Chamus.

7

FOR ANY OTHER MAN to score a pound of uncut heroin, it would have taken a lifetime of securing connections. But for a man like Kenyatta, with friends throughout the world, it took only one phone call and an explanation.

Jackson Mathews, exiled black leader, political radical, and considered an enemy of the American people, had been a true believer, a man who had seen the winds of change coming long before others even knew there was a storm. In the early sixties, he had organized black groups from the West Coast to the East Coast. His basic aim had been to group his black brothers together into one massive army of political

power. He had known that the liberal sensitivity of
the American government would not bring about the
changes. He had also known that the only way to
effect real change was through raw, brutal power.

Only a handful of men in the United States knew
of Mathews' whereabouts, and even fewer had possession of a phone number through which they could
reach him. Kenyatta was one of those men.

Quickly, Kenyatta explained to Mathews in a
coded, jive language what he needed. Mathews agreed
immediately, telling Kenyatta that a shipment would
reach him within two days.

Mathews' connections in the Mediterranean were
such that within an hour he was dealing for a pound
of the white powder. Because of his reputation
amongst the crime syndicates of the European marketplace, the black leader had to set up the score
through a front man, a black who was considered one
of the top drug men in the world but who secretly
worked for Mathews and supplied him with information.

The score was made. The pound of white powder
was being put into a case of French perfumes and
powders, leaving Marseilles on the south coast of
France via freighter to the United States. The contact
was so good that the shipment was being made under
the auspices of a CIA top-secret priority.

In other words, customs and inspection in America
would assume that the box of French perfumes and
powders was a cover, either for a shipment of chem-
icals or possibly a load of film. No matter, the ship-

ment was not to be opened by anyone but the agent involved.

That agent, unknown and unnamed, would meet the freighter at the New York City docks, then deliver the goods to a secluded landing strip in the Adirondack Mountains. There the small parcel would be flown to Los Angeles with a landing at San Fernando Airport in the San Fernando Valley. The little used airstrip would provide the pickup point for Kenyatta.

On Wednesday morning, only four days after the hit on the O.E.O. house, Kenyatta was in possession of a pound of raw, uncut heroin. The arrival of the powder signaled a new era in the black man's methods. As he drove from the airport with the parcel resting on his lap, Kenyatta felt a twinge of disgust.

His hatred of the stuff was something that had driven him through the years, motivating him to strengthen his army, to blast away at the pushers and junkies in the ghettos who were quickly destroying the hope of the black people. Now, the "white devil" powder was in his grasp—over a million dollars street value. Kenyatta chuckled as he realized for the first time the significance of the color of heroin powder.

Johnny Miller sat alone that Wednesday night in the quiet darkness of the Center Club, a rundown beer joint on Compton Boulevard known primarily for its equally rundown junkies and the presence of dime whores. The little black dude sat at the bar nursing a cheap whiskey and listening to the sounds of "Sweets" Edison on the juke.

For four days, Miller had been talking with everyone he knew in the South Central District attempting
to gather as much information as possible on
Kenyatta. The hundred and forty dollars he had scored
from Benson and Ryan had come in handy, bringing
him enough junk to last out the rest of the week. He
wanted more and made every effort to secure information that would bring him some cash from the
Detroit detectives.

But the name Kenyatta was one that was not uttered
in the Los Angeles ghetto. If anyone knew of the black
leader's presence, they weren't talking about it. The
hit on the O.E.O. house had been discussed, and
everyone assumed that it did in fact have something
to do with the Black Maria gang and a vendetta.

The arrest of Lucius Davis and his arraignment the
following Monday on two counts of first-degree murder seemed enough to convince everybody that the
small-time gang lord had been the main man behind
the murder and fire. The other members of the Black
Maria had disappeared quickly, and the talk was concerned mainly with when they would hit again, and
whom.

So the grapevine on the streets had been fruitless
for Miller. He had not picked up on any particular ten-
sions or on the usual calm before the storm when
something big was coming down. Everything seemed
as it should be.

But this Wednesday night was to change all that. It
began with the arrival of Curt Horning, a small-time
dealer in junk and whores who often did a little busi-

ness with Miller. He arrived at the Center Club around nine o'clock and sat down on the stool next to Miller.

"What's happenin', baby?" Horning asked, knocking on the bar twice to get the bartender's attention.

"Not much, man," Miller replied. "Fuckin' quiet out there tonight."

Horning ordered a Jack Daniels—not just a shot but a bottle. "Big time's comin' down, Miller. Big fuckin' time!"

Miller looked at the small, rotund black man who wore expensive double-knits and ascots. He had never known Horning to bullshit. The man was a cynic about his life and always played his honesty to the point of being absurd. He knew that he was small, and he accepted that fact. That is why Miller was so shocked by the man's words.

"What're you tryin' to lay down, Horning?" Miller asked after the smaller black man poured out a shot of the good whiskey for each of them.

"I'm tellin' ya, my man, there's talk out there on the streets. Heard little bits down at Jimmy's pool hall."

Miller grunted. "Shit, man, you know where those dudes are at! Ain't nothin' but one piece of bull after 'nother."

"Yeah," Horning replied, "but it wasn't all there was, man. Heard somethin' from Willis."

Willis was the main information man in the ghetto. The man to whom all the smaller dealers went when they needed a score. Willis took commissions and lived pretty damn well. His job was to keep his fingers on the pulse, know when things were tight and when they were plentiful. If a man didn't know the score, Willie would tell them in no uncertain terms.

"Well?" Miller began, now impatient. "What the fuck did Willis say?"

Horning continued to stare at the wood bar in front of him. He put both hands on the smooth surface and examined his nails as he spoke. "Big shipment, Miller. I mean, really fuckin' big. Came in sometime…maybe this mornin', maybe las' night. No one knows for sure."

Miller felt the excitement growing inside. Shipments of the stuff came into L.A. quietly. Suddenly, they would appear on the streets, with every pusher unloading his bit. The announcement of a large shipment, even the rumor, could mean only one thing. There was someone new; some dude was attempting to break into the LA market.

"How they know?" Miller asked Horning.

"Word from France is what I hear. That's all, you dig? Just word from France."

"Shit, it's not beaner junk?"

"No way," Horning replied. "It's the fine powder. The good stuff, baby. The really fine shit!"

Miller felt himself grow weak. He took a shotful of whiskey and poured it down, letting the warm liquid return some energy to his legs. This was really the big time, he thought, if what Horning was saying was true. Something was going down, and it was bigger than he had feared it would be.

Horning lifted himself off the stool and pushed the

bottle of Jack Daniels across to Miller. "I tol' you this shit, Miller, 'cause if you get any action off the stuff, I expect the favor returned. You dig where I'm comin' from?"

Miller nodded. "You got it, my man. An' I thank you."

Horning nodded and ambled out of the bar like a man who knew the secret of life. As Miller watched him, he realized that quite possibly the short, flabby black man did know—at least the secret to his life.

Detectives Benson and Ryan were spending their Wednesday night poring over the files on Joe Collins at police headquarters.

The mutilated body of Collins had been discovered Monday morning by two black children on their way to grammar school. The sight of the emaciated body had so disturbed the kids that they were now under a doctor's care and staying home from school. When Benson and Ryan had arrived on the scene, both kids were in a state of shock.

One, a little girl of six years, could not speak to the two detectives. She was so terrified that she was virtually gagging on her own vomit.

They had searched the remains of Collins and had found nothing in the way of evidence. The young black's suitcase was lying at the head of the alleyway where he had dropped it. And his jacket lay only a few yards away. Other than that, there was nothing that provided any kind of clue as to who the hit men were.

Lieutenant Stein arrived on the scene only moments after the two Detroit detectives. He had spoken immediately, saying that the killing was only a vendetta action by members of the Black Maria against the man who had taken Elliot Stone from the hospital. The fact that Stone's presence in the hospital had been kept out of the newspapers didn't faze Stein at all. "That," according to the lieutenant, "was Collins' involvement."

Benson disagreed quickly, saying that as far as they knew there was nothing in Collins' background that would even indicate he had been a member of a gang. The young orderly had worked in the hospital since the age of seventeen, being the sole support of his mother after his two brothers were killed in action in Vietnam.

Stein just shrugged his shoulders and glared at Benson. "You're trying to blow up this whole thing," Stein warned. "Then you and your partner'll go back to Detroit, leaving me with a city full of murdering niggers." This time Stein did not hesitate in using the word.

That had been Monday. And since then, Benson and Ryan had become more determined than ever to piece together what was coming down in the City of the Angels. Something was up, and both men felt it. They could not put a finger on it, but they knew that this time Kenyatta had come close to hitting someone's nerve. Three men had died because of it, and there was no telling how many more would get hit before the whole thing was over with.

"Well, that's about enough for me," Ryan said disgustedly as he threw the last portfolio onto the large desk in front of him.

Benson looked up from his wide open folder. "You wanna grab something to eat?"

"Sure, why not."

Before leaving the police headquarters, Benson phoned the Biltmore and checked to see if anyone had left a message. His heart began pumping wildly when he heard the name Miller. "Our man Johnny," Benson said excitedly to Ryan. "He wants to meet."

Ryan contacted Miller, and they planned a meeting in the garage beneath Pershing Square.

One hour later, the three men were sitting in a remote section of the garage inside the detective's unmarked sedan. Miller sat in the rear, nervously puffing on his gold-plated cigarette holder.

"All right, Miller, what's happening?" Ryan began.

Miller took a deep drag on his cigarette, then leaned back in his seat. "Somethin' big is comin' down, gentlemen," he said simply.

"What do you mean, 'somethin' big?'" Benson demanded.

"What I mean, man, is that someone is bringing in a score of junk that's already blowin' everyone's mind. That's what I mean."

"How big?" Ryan asked.

"Don't know. But from the sound of things, it's bigger'n anythin' any dude ever sank into L.A."

"Take a guess, Miller. Quarter, half…, what?"

"Least a half, man. At least!"

Benson glanced at Ryan quickly. They both knew what their next question would be. "And who's bringing it, Miller?" Ryan finally asked.

"That's the part that's got all the dudes unwrapped. We usually got a source down there, dig? I mean, one dude who keeps the junk on the streets—had it together for two, maybe three years now. An' it ain' that dude who's bringin' it, man. It's someone else."

Benson smiled at Ryan. They knew who that dude was and why he was bringing it in. They had discussed the possibility during the last adventure with Kenyatta, wondering when the man would actually get into the marketplace himself. It seemed only a matter of time before Kenyatta would go underground and infiltrate.

"Any idea as to when it came in?" Benson asked.

"People out there suspect within the last twenty-four. But no one's got a handle on it." Miller looked from Ryan to Benson. Obviously he had made some sort of hit.

"That's all you know?" Ryan was already fishing into his pocket for a hundred-dollar bill.

"Yeah. That's the scam. I mean, it appears as though the dude who's had it wired is in for a little competition, if you dig where I'm comin' from."

"No idea who he is, the main man down there?" Benson asked the question casually.

"Man," Miller replied, "ain't no one knows who the cat really is. That dude has it so well put together he probably don't even think he's doin' it himself!"

Miller laughed at his humor, then reached across

the seat and took the bill from Ryan. "If I hear anythin' more, we'll talk again." And with that, the little dapper hustler jumped out of the car and walked quickly toward his late-model Ford parked across the way.

"Shit," Benson said. "It's got to be Kenyatta."

"Uh huh. You think he's in it for the money?"

"Nope. If I know Kenyatta as well as I think I do, the man's a little pissed at whoever knocked over his operation. He's not gonna hit. He's gonna go inside and infiltrate,blow it to pieces from inside."

Ryan looked at Benson before speaking. "You mean, whoever hit his O.E.O. house didn't know what they were hitting?"

"Uh uh. I really don't think anyone knows that Kenyatta's here. I think the cats who made the hit were hitting it for the right reason, only they had no idea who ran it. Probably thought it was a local police operation, undercover or something like that."

"Shit," Ryan exclaimed. "It would be a fucking blessing if we could find out what was going on inside that house."

Elliot Stone limped from the bedroom into the living room. Kenyatta, Rufus, and Edgar were sitting on the floor dividing up a half pound of heroin into small, waterproof bags. Each small bag contained one ounce of the stuff—enough to last a high-shooting junkie for weeks.

"Kenyatta," Stone began, leaning against the bar, "I never thought I'd see that!"

Kenyatta laughed as he tied one small bag and placed it on the stack with the others. "My man, you ain' seen jack shit! No way!"

"You got ahold of Horning yet?" Stone asked.

"Yeah. The fucker's settin' up somethin' for tomorrow night with no other than Chamus."

"Shit, we're movin' in fast!"

Kenyatta held a bag in front of him and turned the small packet over and over in his hands. "Man," he began softly, "with this kind of shit floatin' around, no way them dudes gonna take their time. 'Specially a dude like Chamus!"

Stone poured himself a shot of Jack Daniels and sat easily on one of the stools in front of the bar. His recuperation had amazed everyone, including the doctor. It had only been a few days, and the man was almost whole again. But deep inside, Stone was hurting. He knew Kenyatta was moving into the biggest game he had ever played, and Stone desperately wanted a piece of the action.

The stakes were higher now than they had ever been. But Stone had been known and seen. He would have to sit on the sidelines and watch. It was the first time in his young life that he had ever been made to view the game from the bench.

"You go easy on that whiskey, my man," Kenyatta advised as he joined Stone at the bar.

"It helps," Stone said simply.

"Elliot, you got shit for your pain. 'Nough fuckin' drugs to start your own operation!"

Stone shook his head. "It ain't just the pain,

Kenyatta. You're movin' in like you are, an' I'm fuckin' sittin' here like some kind of wounded man. I just can't dig it."

Kenyatta put his hand on the younger man's shoulder and smiled at him. "Listen, I dig where you're comin' from, baby. I know how you feel, what your gut is tellin' you."

Stone nodded. "Thanks, my man. But it still doesn't come off, dig? I mean, we're sittin' on the biggest motherfucker since we been together. One fuckin' action, one hit, and we clean out the entire community."

"That's right," Kenyatta agreed. "An' that's why it's so important that we keep it cool till we know for sure what's comin' down. You dig?"

"And then what?" Stone asked, looking at Kenyatta with questioning eyes.

Kenyatta returned Stone's gaze directly and cleanly. "You want in on the big hit, don't you?"

"That's where I'm comin' from, Kenyatta."

The tall, bald black man shrugged his massive shoulders, set his glass of whiskey down on the bar, and stared at the pile of heroin sitting in the midst of the living room. "Okay," he began softly. "When we decide to go ahead, you're in. Won't make any difference then, anyway."

Stone smiled. "Thanks, my man."

"Ain't no one better than you, Elliot. No one." Kenyatta spoke softly and with conviction. Stone knew that he meant every word of it..

8

WILBUR CHAMUS, AGE thirty-eight, was a veteran of the Korean war, a former resident of New York City, and now a veteran of the Los Angeles area. He was a black man, a former street hustler, and a pimp, making the big score and rising to the top, now the overseer of twenty separate drug rings in the South Central district of L.A., drug rings that served the junior-high-school crowd up to the serious, lifetime junkies.

The man Wilbur Chamus, better known to his friends as "Slim," stood six feet two inches tall and weighed barely one hundred and fifty pounds. He wore his hair short and sported a finely manicured goatee. His dress habits were perfect—stylized double-knits, leather jackets, and a vast array of expensive hats. He smoked the best Havana cigars and always sported a beautiful black woman wherever he went. To a great many young people in the depressing neighborhoods of Watts, Wilbur Chamus was a man to be admired.

On the Saturday night following the hit of the O.E.O. house, Chamus met with two of his biggest drug traffickers in his office above the Paris Club, which he owned. The two men were Junior Willis and Elmo Zachary, black kingpins in their own right. Wilbur had called the two men to his office because he had been approached through Horning about the possibility of buying a large amount of heroin.

Horning had come to Chamus after being approached himself by Rufus. Kenyatta's man had told the street hustler that his man had scored big and was seeking a buyer. Horning was also told that there was five thousand bucks involved as a finder's fee if the man would set up the buy with Chamus. Horning had agreed instantly to try.

Five thousand was more money than the small-time hustler had ever seen at any one time in his life. As he left Rufus that night, the plump black man chuckled to himself, remembering telling Johnny Miller only hours before about the big times comin' down. They were bigger than Horning ever would have dreamed.

Using his slight knowledge of Chamus' operation, Horning had been able to make contact with the big man through Junior Willis. Willis, who owned a small pawnshop as a front, had been ready to listen. After being told of the stash, Willis had gone directly to Chamus. Now, the three men sat in the office trying to work out the possibilities of what they had learned.

Wilbur Chamus spoke in a high-pitched voice, occasionally growing even higher whenever he became excited. He was excited on this Saturday night, and his voice cracked.

"If we can get the shit at a lower price than Manning delivers," Chamus said, "we'll go."

Junior Willis sat on the expensive couch and sipped at his bourbon and water. He had been listening to the same line for the last three hours, but he still had his doubts. "What you mean," Willis said, "is if we know who the fuck's brought this shit in…, right, my man?"

"Man," Chamus replied, "this can't be no setup. The pigs in this fuckin' town ain't got no access to that much shit. An' if they did, no cop with his head on straight would be usin' it to nail some dudes!"

"I can dig it," Elmo Zachary nodded. "They'd unload the shit themselves…, make some fine fuckin' green."

"Right," Chamus said quickly. "I think we're onto somethin' here…, somethin' big. Man, we get another connection besides that motherfuckin' white honkie Manning, we'll be playin' both sides against the middle!"

Chamus laughed. "If they scorin' that big, my man, then they heard of Wilbur Chamus. You dig where I'm comin' from?" It was always within Chamus'

character to forego safety when in doubt and ratio-
nalize himself to dangerous positions. It was not that
he enjoyed the danger or the uncertainty but because
he was truly conceited about himself and his position
in the underworld. Willis knew it, yet he was powerless to stop him when Chamus got himself hyped.

"Okay, my man, you know where you're comin'
from. I can't say no more." Willis leaned back on the
couch and stared at the glass he held in his hand.

Chamus knew what the man was thinking. But once
again the tall, thin black dealer refused to allow
Willis' questions to penetrate. Chamus had come a
long way and had traveled the rough terrain by himself, without help from outsiders. His judgment, good
or bad, had brought him this far and he wasn't about
to desert it now.

"Willis," Chamus began in a low-keyed voice, "I
don't know who the fuck you think you're dealin'
with, man, but lemme lay somethin' down on your
damned head."

Willis remained seated on the couch, staring at his
half-finished drink. He knew what was coming and
was prepared for it.

Chamus glared at his black hustler for a moment
before beginning. "I'll tell you, Willis," he said. "Ain't
no one in this fuckin' world knows anythin' more
'bout my shit than myself. No one. An' that includes
you, you dig?"

Willis nodded, then took a long swig from his drink.
Chamus stood directly in front of him and stared down
at the black man, hoping to garner some better

response than he had. But Willis refused to budge.

In a brief moment Chamus' urge was to swipe the glass out of Willis' hand, take the smaller man by the lapels, and throw him across the room. But once again, the tall black man managed to control his temper. He knew that any action like that would only mean a tougher time down the road. And with the amount of money that was now at stake, it would be a mistake to jeopardize their future.

Annie's Restaurant was a small, greasy-spoon diner located on Alvarado off Wilshire in downtown Los Angeles. Most of Annie's regular customers were winos, the down-and-out men of the streets. There was no racial imbalance inside the garishly-lit room. Both blacks and whites were accepted.

Junior Willis stood out amongst the poorly-dressed men with his mohair suit, trim tie, and alligator shoes. His tall, lean frame seemed to dominate the small diner when he entered. Quickly, he took a seat at the counter and ordered a cup of coffee.

Two country-and-western tunes later, Willis was joined at the counter by Horning. The small, heavy-set black man was excited, his eyes bulging with interest as he waited for Willis' reply.

"Well?" Horning asked quietly after a long silence.

"You got it, my man," Willis replied quietly.

"You mean we're goin' with it?"

"That's right, Horning. Just spoke with the man a few minutes ago. We set it up with equal men on both sides. No guns and a chemist that my man will supply."

Horning stared down at his coffee for a moment. "What's in it for me?"

"You jivin' me?" Willis snapped.

"Man," Horning pleaded, "we ain't got down to no talkin' that I can recall."

Willis sighed. "All right, my man. Two percent of the sale. That 'nough for you?"

Horning could not control the smile that etched its way across his face. Two percent of a million was a lot of cash. More bread than the little black man ever thought he would see. "Okay, Willis," Horning replied, "you got yourself a deal. I'll call you as soon as I see my man."

The two men shook hands as Horning rose from his stool. The smaller man was happy, excited about his prospects, but as he looked into Willis' face, a sudden tremor of fear surged through him. The money sounded good, was good, but there was something else happening here that Horning could not quite grasp. As he left Willis sitting alone at the counter, Horning kept telling himself that his fears were coming from the fact that now he was dealing in the big time, and at that altitude every man suffered.

The Los Angeles night was hot and clear. Horning drove his old, beat-up Chevy through the downtown area and continued on through the city center towards Watts. He had done his job, and from now on he hoped that he could just go back and collect his money. He would tell the tall, bald-headed supplier named Jim that the arrangements had been made and everything was ready to go. That dude, thought Horning, envisioning the massive size of the man named Jim, is one hell of a fucker.

Horning had met Kenyatta just that one night, only twenty hours before, when Rufus had approached him. They had gone together to a small apartment on Fifty-fourth Street, a place rented by Kenyatta just for this occasion. There, with Rufus and Edgar standing watch and Elliot Stone looking from the bedroom, Kenyatta, known to Horning as "Jim," had laid it down.

"We know you got motherfuckin' good connections in this town," Kenyatta had said, watching Horning closely. "An' we intend to use them."

Horning had sipped on his Jack Daniels and listened quietly as Kenyatta explained to him just how big a deal it was that was coming down. Without mentioning specifics, Kenyatta told him that all of the South Central area could be taken care of for at least six months with the amount of stuff in Kenyatta's possession. After explaining it all to Horning, the room had fallen into silence as the men waited for the small black man's answer.

"I think," Horning began slowly, feeling the tension rise in himself, "that I can help."

Kenyatta smiled. His organization had known about Horning for a long time, had seen him work the streets and sometimes make a big score with one of the larger dealers. They had known that he had an inside track to Chamus. Now, they were taking a chance, that the little man's sources were as good as they believed.

"Who is the dude?" Kenyatta asked after pouring another round.

Horning laughed nervously. "Aw, man, you know I can't lay that jive down on you...."

"Sure, man. Okay. Just set it up, and we'll meet."

They spoke for another hour and finally agreed to a one-percent cut of the selling price. It was an unwritten law among the big dealers that the middle man got a cut from each side without divulging his take to anyone. Now, Horning was in on three percent—a healthy cut.

Horning turned slowly onto Fifty-fourth Street and pulled to a stop in front of the modern-looking apartment house. Palm trees swayed in the wind outside, and Horning listened as he heard the laughter of party-goers in an apartment upstairs. In his mind, he saw the day when he had money and would be able to party like the people upstairs. Throughout Horning's life, that had been his ultimate goal—a little bread, some fine women, and a whole lot of liquor. Outside of that, nothing much interested the short, plump black man.

After knocking three times on the door, Horning waited. He heard the sound of footsteps inside, then someone coming to the door. In a moment, Rufus swung open the door. "Hey, man, what's happenin'?" Rufus asked, his drawl much thicker than usual.

"Got to talk with Jim, man," Horning said.

Rufus grinned and winked at Horning as he stood aside and let the smaller man into the living room. The apartment was just the same as when Horning had seen it the night before—a sofa, three chairs, and

a small coffee table; the kitchen off to the side sported a stand-up bar, and that was about it. Horning knew
that, when men dealt with the kind of stash these guys
did, the simpler things were the easier and safer the
sale would be.

Kenyatta entered the room after Horning had taken
a seat on the couch. He was wearing a turtleneck and
tight-fitting pants. He looked bigger than Horning had
remembered, and somehow much more threatening.

"Well, my man. What's jivin'?"

Horning took a deep breath before speaking. He
looked up quickly at Rufus leaning against the door,
then back at Kenyatta. "Jim," he began, "they want
to deal."

Kenyatta glanced at Rufus and smiled. "See, man.
I tol' you this little dude was goin' come out all right.
He's our man."

"Yeah, baby," Rufus exclaimed, "the cat's straight."

It should have come off as a compliment to
Horning, but instead he felt a cold chill of suspicion
run up his spine. Something wasn't quite right, and
he was beginning to feel it.

"Man," Kenyatta began again, "you goin' be one
rich sonofabitch. Can you dig that, Horning?"

The small black man nodded. The thought of the
money had left him for a moment, but now it took
center place in his mind. He realized that all thoughts
he might have, all paranoid feelings, were due to the
fact that he was dealing with such high stakes. This
was no street gig this time, he told himself.

Kenyatta poured a drink for Horning, then for Rufus

and himself. As he handed the drink to Horning he asked, "All right, man, what's the gig?"

"Well, Jim," Horning began, "he wants a meeting. Two of your people, two of his. And a chemist, some dude to analyze the shit."

"Sounds righteous," Kenyatta replied. "Anything else, my man?"

"Uh, yeah. No guns."

"That go both ways?" Kenyatta asked.

"Yeah, no shit, man. It's straight." Horning took a quick sip of his drink.

"Okay. Set it up. Make the arrangements for the place and the time. We bring a sample, enough to analyze, then we talk a little 'bout the business. You dig?"

Horning nodded. "I'll get back to him tonight. Should have somethin' happenin' later."

Kenyatta reached down and patted Horning on the shoulder. The little man seemed to collapse inside himself, withdraw into a shell. Kenyatta knew the man was dealing outside his league, and he also knew that, if the deal was to succeed, Horning would have to have confidence. "My man," Kenyatta began softly, "you bring this thing off for us, and I'll take you in with me. We need a dude who can think, an' I can see that you ain't much for action. Think about it, Horning, and remember you got yourself a place here. You dig where I'm comin' from?"

Horning looked up and smiled. "Yeah, and thanks, man."

"Don't mention it, baby. We're all in the same fuckin' game together."

After Horning left, Kenyatta watched him through the window. "That little dude's gonna get himself cut real bad before this gig is through."

Elliot Stone entered the room, looking now as though he had done nothing more than fall down a porch step. He was moving well, and his old agility seemed to have returned. "It's goin' down, eh?" he asked.

Kenyatta turned from the window. "That's right. Once we get through that Horning, we're goin' right to the top. They're interested and, if Chamus feels that way, then the dudes he's been dealin' with are gonna feel the same fuckin' way."

Stone leaned against the bar and lit a cigarette. "How you goin' to get through Chamus? I mean, he's a big, mean cat with lots of local connections. You dig where it's at?"

"Yeah, I dig, Elliot. The way I see it, though, we got ourselves a couple of ways to go with this thing. A little muscle in the right place or we tell him we got in our possession one little fuckin' file. Enough to rip apart his entire organization if it was to get into the wrong hands."

"Man," Stone replied, "I don' know 'bout that. I mean, you're puttin' yourself awfully close to me. You know that?"

"Sure, man," Kenyatta said. "But I don't think we'll have to worry about that. Rufus here, and Edgar, they both handle themselves pretty fuckin' well. I think in that meetin' we'll just need the muscle. Not much else."

Stone nodded. He hoped that Kenyatta was right. But then again, if Chamus knew that Kenyatta had the file, Stone would be able to surface again and get in on the action himself. But that was only wishful thinking, and Stone knew it.

One hour passed, and finally the phone call came from Horning. At six o'clock that morning they were to meet with *the man* at Weldon's warehouse, a broken-down building on Adams Boulevard near Crenshaw. In a nervous voice Horning explained how the signals were to work and what they were to do when they arrived. When he finished, Kenyatta complimented him on his efficiency and Horning responded with a crisp "thanks," the kind that men utter when they know that, no matter how well they do, they are going to lose anyway.

After hanging up the phone, Kenyatta turned to Stone and Rufus. "Well, gentlemen," he said, "break out the Jack Daniels. Looks like we're goin' to have one long motherfucker tonight!"

Weldon's warehouse was dark at five minutes to six that morning. The street running along the south wall was empty except for an occasional wild dog roaming the gutters looking for food. The tall, two-story building stood between an empty lot on one side and a deserted factory on the other.

Rufus drove the big Cadillac slowly in front of the wooden warehouse, then turned the corner after the factory. Kenyatta sat in front, peering silently at the dark shadows and the empty terrain. Behind him

Edgar sat tensely waiting, holding a small satchel that contained one ounce of pure, uncut heroin.

Behind the warehouse was an alleyway. Rufus pulled into the small opening and cruised slowly until he reached the rear loading dock of the warehouse. There a white light bulb burned above the platform. When the front bumper of the Cadillac was parallel to the end of the platform, the light suddenly went out.

"That's our signal, gentlemen," Kenyatta said coldly.

Rufus nodded as he pulled the car to a stop just beyond the platform. "Well, let's make it in and have our visit," he said.

"Remember," Kenyatta began before either Rufus or Edgar could get out of the car. "Elliot and his men are just outside, in front. If this is some kind of motherfuckin' setup, go that way."

"Man," Edgar replied, "you best believe I haven't forgotten that shit!"

Kenyatta nodded, opened his door, and climbed out. He stretched his tense body in the early morning chill, but the cold was not affecting him. His adrenaline had been flowing all night, waiting for the chance to deal with Chamus. It had been a year in coming, and now he was about to break it open.

Or at least he hoped he was. He knew what the danger would be inside since no one was supposed to be carrying weapons, and he hoped that none of Chamus' men had black belts in karate. Kenyatta, Edgar, and Rufus had black belts themselves, but only a handful

of men had ever seen them use it. And they were now
dead.

Rufus and Edgar joined Kenyatta, taking their
stance on either side of the tall black man. "Okay,"
Kenyatta said, "you fuckers remember my name is
Jim, dig?"

Rufus chuckled. With everything that was going
down, Kenyatta's biggest worry all night had been
whether or not the two men would blow the name.

The three men approached the platform slowly.
Suddenly, out of the shadows, appeared a tall, heavyset black man wearing an old army jacket. "It ain't
dawn yet," he said.

"Yeah," Kenyatta replied, "but it's cool."

The man nodded and waited as Kenyatta and his
two men climbed the stairs and joined him on the
dock. Without speaking, the heavyset black opened
the small door to the warehouse and stood aside as
Kenyatta and his men walked through.

The inside of the building was cold and damp. The
smell of rotting wood permeated everything. Kenyatta
stood in the hallway, lit only by one naked bulb, and
waited. Rufus and Edgar were right behind him.
Finally, at the other end, a medium-sized black man
wearing a business suit and a huge fur coat over that
approached the trio.

"This way," he said simply. Kenyatta and his men
followed the black down the hallway to the end, where
they turned a corner and entered through the first door
on the right.

"Gentlemen," the black said, "welcome."

Inside the small office sat Wilbur Chamus, wearing a huge coat and a felt hat. To either side of him stood the largest black men Kenyatta had ever seen. Both men wore turtlenecks and light windbreakers. Kenyatta knew instantly that they were dressed for action.

The large table in the center of the room provided the neutral ground for the meeting. Chamus gestured to the chair opposite him, and Kenyatta took a seat.

"How's it goin', man?" Chamus asked lightly, looking directly at Kenyatta.

"Everythin' seems to be cookin', my man."

"That's cool," Chamus replied softly. "Hard times we got happenin' 'round abouts."

Kenyatta smiled, a crooked, effortless grin that had brought fear to many a man. "You look like you doin' all right, though."

Chamus laughed, a high-pitched giggle that sounded more nervous than humorous. "That's right, Jim. A man learns who his friends are, and he makes things happen. You dig where I'm comin' from?"

Kenyatta nodded.

The two men sat facing each other for a moment longer. Chamus was attempting to size up this strange black man who had come into Los Angeles with a pound of heroin and a willingness to deal. He realized that there were many questions still not answered, but he also realized what kind of money was at stake here. He would answer those questions later. For now, the huge, bald black man sitting opposite him was his key to a fortune.

And Kenyatta stared into the face of Wilbur Chamus. The man seemed etched in time and place, as though he had never been a child and had always looked the way he did now. His bony face and cold eyes gave away nothing, Kenyatta decided. Nothing at all. The only way to tell if something was coming down with the man was through his voice. Kenyatta decided that he had better listen intently to the tone of Chamus' voice. It was the only way to read the man.

"You wanna get your shit?" Chamus asked after a brief silence.

Edgar pulled out the small baggie of white powder from the satchel and passed behind Kenyatta with it. As he gave the heroin to Stewart, he felt all eyes in the room on him.

Kenyatta watched the men across the table from him intensely. He had heard of the magic of the powder but had never seen its effects this close at hand. Like a magical metal, the men were drawn to the stuff—worshipful of it even. Kenyatta looked from Chamus to his bodyguards and back to Chamus again. He wished that he could kill all three on the spot, but he knew that he must wait.

Stewart took the small bagful of smack and walked back into the room with it. Kenyatta watched him close the door behind him, then turned back to Chamus. "I know," Kenyatta said, "that the little white friend in there ain't gonna do nothin' stupid. Ain't worth but a couple thou' out on the streets. You dig where I'm comin' from?"

Chamus frowned at Kenyatta. "Man, I am the main man in Los Angeles. No way I'd pull anythin' like snatchin' your little bit of stash. You dig? I mean, you deal with me, baby, and you deal with the biggest!"

"Right on!" Kenyatta replied, amazed at the man's ego. It wasn't everyone, he thought, who would come out and admit something like that to a total stranger. Buying was one thing, but letting a dude in on your game was another.

They waited for fifteen minutes while the chemist tested the purity of the heroin inside the other room. Kenyatta smoked a cigarette, and Chamus busied himself with a cigar. Finally, Stewart emerged from the room. He was smiling. Kenyatta could see that the little white man never enjoyed disappointing people.

"Okay, Stewart, what's happenin'?" Chamus asked, his voice high-pitched.

"Well," Stewart began, "the stuff is the best I've ever seen, Mister Chamus. The very best!"

Chamus looked at Stewart for a moment longer, then glanced quickly at Kenyatta. "He seems to dig your smack, Jim baby."

"Ain't no reason he shouldn't, my man," Kenyatta replied. "The stuff is as good as it comes."

Chamus smiled quickly. He told Stewart to leave, and the white man hurried out of the office quickly. Kenyatta wondered where little white men like Stewart went when they were finished serving black men like Chamus. Probably some little room with flowers and a television set, Kenyatta thought.

"Okay, my man," Chamus began in earnest. "We

know the stuff is fine, but we ain't sure which batch this shit is from. So, when we deal and make the exchange, we bring Stewart along again just to keep things honest. You dig?"

"Yeah, only one thing we ain't got to yet, Chamus," Kenyatta said. "We ain't talked 'bout why we're both in this motherfuckin' cold warehouse when we should be home in bed with a foxy lady. Man, we ain't talked money. You dig that?"

Chamus laughed. "Oh, man, what I'm goin' offer you ain't gonna do nothin' but make your head swim!"

Kenyatta grinned at Chamus. "Okay, my man. I'm waitin'."

Chamus leaned back in his chair and puffed smoothly on his cigar. The game was his, or so he thought, and no one was going to stop him now. "Jim, my man, you deliver me a pound of that shit, as right-eous as the shit we seen here this mornin', and I'm prepared to grease your palm with a cool million. In cash, small bills, and none marked. Can you dig that?"

Kenyatta stared at Chamus coldly. The other man's eyes began to grow hazy. He had expected a little more than just a leveled stare.

"What is it with you, my man?" Chamus demand-ed.

"A million, eh?"

"That's right."

Kenyatta pulled out a cigarette and lit it slowly. He took a long drag and blew the smoke across the table and into Chamus' face. Both of the black dealer's bodyguards took a threatening step forward. "My man," Kenyatta began slowly, "you tell me you the big man down here. The main man. Well, a dude who can score as big as I do, well, he knows a few things."

Chamus listened in silence, now leaning forward.

"See, my man," Kenyatta continued, "I happen to know you score outside the city, and with people capable of handling what I can deliver."

Tension began filling the room as Chamus ground out his cigar on the table. His anger was rising quickly.

"Now," Kenyatta said, "since I don't know the dudes personally and you do, maybe we can work somethin' out. You dig where I'm comin' from?"

Chamus took a deep breath. When he spoke, his voice was pitched very high. "Man, you got to be somethin' else! You think I...."

Kenyatta cut him off. "Listen, my man. You offer a mil for this shit. Those boys you deal with, they'll go two. Maybe three. Now, man, think! A finder's fee...that's ten percent. Man, that's two, three hundred thou. An' for nothin'!"

"Nothin'?" Chamus screamed. "I offer you a good deal, and now you want somethin' else...."

Kenyatta watched the man as he carried on. He knew that all Chamus was worried about was the five, six-million-dollar profit he could make out on the streets. It was driving him crazy to think it might be slipping through his fingers. Finally, Chamus made his offer once again, this time raising the figure by half a million. Kenyatta just laughed.

"Man, I don't need your fuckin' money! But I do need your contacts an' I'm willin' to pay for them!"

Chamus stared at Kenyatta as though unable to believe what he was hearing. Finally, he sighed, then leaned back in his chair. His voice had dropped when he spoke, and Kenyatta realized the man was up to something when he said, "Okay, man, lemme think on it for a time. Got to talk to some people, you dig?"

"Sure, man, sure. I can dig somethin' like this takin' a little time. But not too much time, you dig?" Kenyatta smiled at Chamus.

"Yeah, I dig it, Jim," Chamus said. He stood up and extended his hand. "Sorry, man, but I didn't see what you were drivin' at, you know. Sometimes a man gets a little hard in the head."

The sudden reversal was too obvious. Kenyatta shook the man's hand and wondered when the truth was going to strike.

Kenyatta, Rufus, and Edgar walked out of the small office. Chamus and his two bodyguards were standing behind the wooden table watching them closely.

The long hallway was empty. The men who were present when Kenyatta had entered the warehouse were now gone.

Kenyatta stopped midway down the hall and turned to Rufus and Edgar. "You guys in the mood for a little action?" he asked.

Both men nodded.

"I think we're goin' get a little outside." Kenyatta led the way. When he reached the door leading out onto the platform, he opened it slowly. The Cadillac was still where he had left it, and the alley was empty. "Okay, be ready," Kenyatta said as he stepped out onto the platform.

The three men walked down the steps and headed toward the Caddy. When they were fifteen feet from the car, the two bodyguards who had been inside the office, along with the two men who had greeted Kenyatta earlier, popped up from behind the car.

"What's happenin'?" Kenyatta asked.

The four black men approached Kenyatta, Rufus, and Edgar slowly. They were unarmed but wore faces thath seemed etched with the approaching violence.

Kenyatta stopped in his tracks. He turned quickly back toward the platform and to Chamus standing above him leaning against the wall. "Well, some kind of shit, man!" Kenyatta said.

Chamus laughed. "My man, I am just tryin' to convince you that you should deal with me. Business tactics, you might say."

Kenyatta laughed in return. The four men were facing his group, their fists clenched at their sides. By their stance, Kenyatta could tell that they were not martial-arts fighters but straight-ahead street punchers. As far as he was concerned, the fight was over before it began. His only problem now would be to get it over with quick enough so that he could land Chamus. He had to get the man himself.

"Okay," Kenyatta said, "have it your way...." At that moment, the bald-headed black man backed into three-point stance, stepped quickly between the two bodyguards, and took both men out with a chop and

a kick. The closed-fist chop struck the man to
Kenyatta's left in the neck, and the sickening sound
of bones being broken filled the early morning air.
The man crumpled to the ground, screaming for his
life.

The kick got the other man directly in the balls.
Kenyatta knew he had broken the man's pelvis as he
felt the bones splinter beneath the heel of his boot.
The man doubled over, grabbed his destroyed sex, and
rolled forward. His groans were muffled, and the black
bile that formed at the corners of his mouth drooled
down his chin.

The moment Kenyatta had struck, Rufus and Edgar
had also moved into action. Rufus took his man with
a quick kick to the hip and a left-handed karate chop
to the man's ribs. Later, the man would count six broken ribs and a dislocated hip. His services were lost
the moment Rufus struck.

Edgar's man had been more difficult. He had seen
Kenyatta strike and had flung out at Edgar with a
right, catching the thin black man across the lower
jaw. Falling onto his back, Edgar raised his legs and
waited for the black hood to jump him. The man came
straight at him, and Edgar grabbed his neck between
his ankles and flung him over onto his side. Jumping
to his feet, Edgar took his foot, placed it on the man's
Adam's apple, and exerted pressure.

The black man died instantly as Edgar pushed his
Adam's apple to the back of his throat. As the man
died, he pissed in his pants and excreted. Bile flew
from his mouth like vomit, and his eyes rolled ba

into his head. Edgar leaned over the man's face and let go himself, allowing a flow of murky vomit to cascade down across the black man's contorted face. It was a sickening sight.

Kenyatta allowed the feeling of pride to swell inside his chest as he surveyed the scene. One man dead, three crippled for life. The black leader had taught his followers well, and it was at times like these that those hours of practice paid off.

The sound of the warehouse door slamming quickly brought Kenyatta out of his thoughts. "Chamus!" he cried, pointing to the closed door. "Rufus, Edgar, c'mon!!!"

The two men hurried up the steps. The back door to the building had been locked by the fleeing dope pusher. Kenyatta took a step back from the door, set himself, then snapped his foot out at the rotting wood with blinding speed. The old door splintered into a million pieces, leaving a gaping hole. Kenyatta reached inside, grabbed the knob, and opened the door.

"He can't make it too far!" Kenyatta exclaimed as he and Edgar raced down the hallway. "Stone's out front...."

Elliot Stone sat low in the front seat of the Ford, directly across the street from the warehouse. He watched the large front of the building closely, his eyes riveted mainly on the door.

When he had arrived three minutes after Kenyatta, Stone had seen the old Plymouth pull to a stop down

the street and around the corner from him. The huge
fins of the automobile stuck out just enough so that
he knew the car was still parked. As far as he could
tell, there were only two men inside.

The order from Kenyatta was for Stone to remain
parked in front of the warehouse until he saw
Kenyatta's Cadillac leave. But that had been over a
half hour ago that he had arrived, and the black athlete was getting fidgety.

Inside the warehouse, Kenyatta and Edgar walked
quietly through the darkened aisles, straining to hear
some sound from the fleeing man, but they heard nothing. The old building was dark, and the only light
came through the slats at the top of the building.
Kenyatta knew the man was still somewhere inside
the building, and that he was playing a waiting game.

Rufus crept up behind the two men carrying two
.38s, one in each hand. He gave the weapons to
Kenyatta and Edgar.

"Any sign?" Rufus asked in a whisper.

"The dude has vanished...," Kenyatta replied. "But
he's still in here."

"Think he's armed?" Rufus asked.

"No way. Would have used it outside if he was."

The three men stood in the center of the huge building, each man facing a different direction. They listened and they waited.

Outside, Elliot Stone peered intently at the building. He felt inside that something was wrong.
Suddenly, a small door near the end of the building
began to open slowly.

Stone reached inside the glove compartment and pulled out his .45. He held the heavy pistol in his right hand, the barrel pointing at an angle toward the ceiling.

The door opened a little farther, and a man peered out wearing a felt hat. Stone recognized him instantly. "Chamus," he said softly to himself, as he gripped the .45 and pulled the hammer back.

Wilbur Chamus bolted from the door, ran down the sidewalk, and turned the corner.

Stone reached for the ignition key and started the engine. He never took his eyes off the tail fins of the Plymouth still visible around the corner.

As he started to pull away from the curb, Stone jammed on the brakes. Suddenly, the Plymouth began backing up. In another moment the entire car was visible. Stone could see the head of Chamus looking around nervously from the backseat.

"Goddamn nigger," Stone cursed. He watched as the car backed up all the way to the opposite side of the street, then the driver turned the wheel hard and peeled out down the street toward Stone.

Stone grabbed the steering wheel, pulled it with all his might to the right, waited for the approaching Plymouth, then stomped on the accelerator. The Ford stalled for a moment, then picked up and careened out into the middle of the street.

The Plymouth was ten feet away when the Ford blocked its way. The driver pulled hard to the right but could not avoid slamming into the rear fender of the Ford.

Before Chamus or his two men inside the Plymouth knew what was happening, Stone was out of his car, his .45 leveled at the three men inside.

"Kill the motherfucker!!!" Chamus screamed, his voice so high it sounded like a wounded animal.

Stone saw the passenger reach inside his coat. Without hesitating he pulled the trigger on his pistol and watched in horror as the glass shattered. The black man's face disappeared in an orgy of blood and bone as the slug entered him just above the nose and between the eyes. Stone whirled and fired one second later at the driver. This time the bullet entered the man's eye, and like an exploding red rose, blew out his eyeball and brains at the same moment.

Chamus had disappeared inside the car. Stone held the gun at arm's length, aiming into the car. The two dead men in the front seat were plastered against the upholstery, their heads barely recognizable as human.

Kenyatta heard the first crash of the cars and began racing toward the front of the warehouse. When he, Rufus, and Edgar reached the door, they heard the two gunshots. For a moment, Kenyatta felt sick to his stomach. His first thought was that Elliot Stone had been gunned down in the waiting car.

"Shit!!!" Kenyatta said, keeping himself and his men inside.

"No sounds, man," Rufus said. "It can't be Elliot."

Kenyatta knew he was right. Quickly, he opened the door and was greeted with the sight of Stone standing like a statue, holding his gun toward the wrecked Ford.

Kenyatta ran out and came up next to Stone. "Shit, Elliot, where's Chamus?" he demanded.

"Don't know, man," Elliot replied, his voice shaking with excitement. "He was in the motherfuckin' car!"

Kenyatta smiled to himself, raised his .38, and walked slowly around the side of the car. He passed the front seat, then peered into the rear.

There on the backseat lay Wilbur Chamus, big-time pusher of heroin to the kids, the junkies, and the whores of Watts. The man lay curled up in the seat, his knees up to his chin and his hands around his legs. He was shaking like a little child. Brain matter and blood from the two dead men up front were all over him, some of it on his face and lips. He had been vomiting, and his face was covered with his own vomit.

"Man," Kenyatta said bitterly, "you are some kind of motherfucker."

Chamus flinched, then turned and looked up at Kenyatta. The man's eyes were like marbles, large and unseeing. "Don't shoot," he begged, his voice like a little girl's.

"Get out!" Kenyatta ordered.

Chamus lay there, not moving.

Kenyatta turned to Stone, who was now standing beside him. "Elliot, get the fuckin' Caddy and bring it around. We got to get out of here!"

Stone ran at full speed to the rear of the warehouse and jumped inside the car. The bodies of the four men lay next to it, and their stench of bile, excrement, and death hovered heavily in the alleyway.

"All right, motherfucker," Kenyatta demanded when Stone had brought the car around, "get the fuck outta there! 'Less you want a bullet down your shit-ass mouth!"

Chamus rolled off the seat, then crawled along the floor and fell out onto the pavement. Rufus and Edgar each grabbed an arm and threw the terrified man into the backseat of the Cadillac.

Kenyatta got into the front with Stone and they drove off. The massacre they left behind would be found within another ten minutes by an aged wino who had been sleeping behind some trash cans in the alley. The man, his brain rotted with the juice, would be able to do one thing for the police—identify the tall, bald-headed black man.

9

AT THE MOMENT THE massacre was taking place at the warehouse, Detectives Ryan and Benson were standing on the lot where the charred remains of the O.E.O. office lay. The FBI agents, still on the scene rummaging through the debris, had made a find. They had called Lieutenant Stein and informed him of their discovery—a small strongbox imbedded in the wall containing a file. Stein had come down to the house alone, without notifying Benson and Ryan.

Agent Comstock, the black man who had met with Ryan and Benson that first day, had spoken with Stein as two of his men attempted to pry open the small strongbox. The problem was that the metal was so twisted from the heat that the normal method of prying was impossible. In order not to destroy the contents of the box, the agents virtually had to chip away at the metal piece by piece.

As Stein watched the operation with Comstock, his face was glum and his brow furrowed. Comstock noticed this and asked the lieutenant if anything was wrong. The white officer shrugged his shoulders and shook his head.

"Where's those two cops from Detroit?" Comstock asked Stein.

"Out on a lead, I think," Stein replied, looking quickly at the black agent.

"They were staying at the Biltmore, weren't they?" Comstock asked.

"Uh huh," Stein replied, staring intently at the men who were attempting to open the box.

Comstock watched the big lieutenant carefully. He had disliked the man since the day he had been brought into the case. There was something unprofessional about him, something that did not jibe with a police officer. And now, when the possibility of a clue was present, he had not bothered to contact the two detectives. To Comstock, this kind of lapse was intolerable and inexcusable.

"Listen, man," Comstock said after a few minutes of silence, "I'm going over to the cafe for some coffee. You stay nearby and keep an eye on things, all right?"

"Sure, Comstock," Stein agreed immediately.

Comstock left the scene, jogging across the street

and around the corner to the small cafe. Inside, he went directly to the phone booth and got the number of the Biltmore Hotel from the information operator.

Benson answered the phone and listened as Comstock explained what was going on at the site. After hanging up the phone, the black FBI agent began to sense that what he was feeling was correct. There was something about Stein that he did not like.

Detectives Benson and Ryan arrived at the site ten minutes after Comstock's call. They lied to Lieutenant Stein, telling him that they had checked in with headquarters and discovered the call that Comstock had made an hour before.

"I had Sergeant Collins ring you guys at the hotel," Stein complained, "but he wasn't able to get in touch."

Benson nodded. "Yeah, well, can never tell about those desk boys. Their heads are always somewhere else."

The two detectives stood for a moment looking into the burnt frame of the house. Comstock ran up to them the moment he saw them, and the two black men confronted each other directly.

"Glad you're here, gentlemen," Comstock said. "We're about ready to break it open. Don't have any idea yet what's inside, but it might help."

Benson nodded to the agent. "Thanks. Sure it's worth a short ride, anyway."

The three men walked through the debris and toward the rear of the burnt house. There, two agents were kneeling over a small metal strongbox. One man held the box while the other jammed a screwdriver into the small opening between the lid and the case. With a grunt, the agent pulled on the screwdriver, and the top of the box snapped open.

"Finally," Comstock said. "We been hacking this thing for over an hour. Didn't want to destroy anything inside."

The three men knelt down around the small box. Comstock pulled out a pair of tweezers from his coat pocket and began lifting the pieces of paper from inside the box. After about twenty sheets, he came to a small packet with the name of a photography laboratory on the outside. He lifted this out of the box and laid it on the ground next to the sheets of paper.

Detective Benson read each typewritten page carefully, passing it on to Ryan when he finished. Then, after reading all of the written contents, he had Comstock pull out the photos from the packet. The agent spread the pictures on the ground in a small circle around the papers. The three men sat on their haunches and looked at the photos.

"Shit," Benson said, "I think we just solved it."

"Looks that way," Comstock said.

"Wilbur Chamus...." Ryan pronounced the name again, then continued. "This is what Stone and the office were doing."

Benson chuckled. "Exactly. Kenyatta's whole thing—break down the pushers, the large rings bringing smack into the ghettos. He must have been about ready to hit Chamus, and Chamus knew it."

"I got to say one thing for this Kenyatta," Comstock said. "He certainly is thorough. He's got enough on this guy to put him away for life."

Suddenly one of the typewritten sheets of paper caught Benson's attention. He picked up the paper and read aloud. "We know there is a contact within the Los Angeles Police Department. An officer. Chamus' street pushers, even though picked up, never spend more than an hour or two in jail. Never prosecuted, and all charges dropped."

The three men looked at each other. "Can you beat that?" Comstock said.

"There's more," Benson said, reading on. "He talks here about a white man…, a certain connection from outside the city. Then he says the operation must be huge, with inroads into organized crime. Jesus!"

The three men stood and stared down at the evidence on the ground at their feet. "Cannot believe this," Comstock said slowly. "We've got ourselves onto something really big here."

"Yeah," Benson agreed. "But so has Kenyatta and he's still one step ahead of us."

At that moment, Lieutenant Stein joined the group of men. For some reason, they all stopped talking and began picking up the contents of the strongbox.

"Find anything?" Stein asked.

"Not much," Comstock replied. "Just a bunch of junk. You know, personal papers, stuff like that."

Benson watched Stein closely. The white officer was vague and seemingly uninterested in a matter that any officer worth his badge should have been. "You wanna take a look?" Benson asked the lieutenant.

"Yeah, sure…, okay," Stein replied.

They watched as Stein leafed through the contents of the strongbox. Finally, he put the papers down. Beads of perspiration had formed on the man's pink forehead. His body seemed to be breaking out in a strong sweat. "Looks good," he mumbled.

Ryan nodded. "Sure as hell does, Stein."

Suddenly, the lieutenant turned on his heels, said something about making a report back at headquarters, and walked quickly toward his car. Comstock, Benson, and Ryan watched him as he jumped into his unmarked car and sped off.

"What do you think?" Benson asked.

"I think," Comstock said slowly, "that we got ourselves a real case."

The conversation was disrupted by an excited uniformed officer who ran across to the burnt house shouting to the officers that a full-scale massacre had taken place only three miles away.

Before leaving the site, Benson quickly packed the strongbox and held it close to his body as he ran toward his car to join Ryan.

Neighborhood children had gathered behind and in front of the abandoned warehouse. The little black kids dressed in torn and tattered clothes and some of the older boys wearing colorful beanies milled around the squad cars and ambulances. They were silent as they looked down upon the mangled bodies. Blood was everywhere, still seeping from the dead men.

Ryan, Benson, and Comstock pulled up to the site and were signaled through by the uniformed officer.

The entire block had been sealed off by the police. News crews with their cameras humming were at that moment still trying to break through.

They came upon the Plymouth, still sitting in the middle of the street with the two dead men in the front seat. Their already rotting bodies were covered with flies and the stench of death.

"Has anyone run a make on the license number yet?" Benson asked the uniformed policeman standing next to the car.

"Yes. We're still waiting," he answered.

Ryan walked to the front of the car and noticed the dent on the right fender and the black paint that must have come from the other car. He called Comstock over and asked if their men could run a lab check on the paint. Comstock jotted down the request in a small black book.

Sergeant Harry Clemmens, a thin white man with a huge mustache and very little hair, approached Benson and Ryan. "You guys Benson and Ryan from Detroit?" Clemmens asked gruffly.

"That's right," Benson answered, staring into the officer's clear, cold blue eyes.

"I called you both. We got a witness in the alley, an old wino who fits the description of the black you're looking for."

"Now, Willie," Clemmens began, addressing the old man slowly and kindly, "tell these two men here what you saw this morning."

Willie swung his feet over the edge of the platform and looked to Benson. "Got a cigarette, man?" he asked in a hoarse, wine-soaked voice.

"Sure, man," Benson said, pulling out a Pall Mall and handing it to the wino. Willie shook as he placed the cigarette between his lips and used both hands to keep the cigarette steady while Benson lit it for him.

"Now, Willie, my man," Benson began, dropping his voice into street slang, "tell us what you saw. It's very important."

Willie drew heavily on his cigarette, then spoke. "Well, I wuz sleepin'…behind them trash cans. I hear a car pull up an' stop, ya know? Couple of dudes get out…."

"What color were they, Willie?" Benson interrupted.

"Jeez, man, what other color come down heah but black? Those men were niggers, man." Willie seemed to glare at the black detective as though the man was incapable of understanding something that was very simple.

"Now," Benson began, "could you describe the man?"

"Sure, man," Willie replied. "He was the biggest fuckin' nigger I ever seen. I mean huge. An' he was bald, completely bald. He was mean, man, really mean!"

Benson and Ryan exchanged glances. "Let's get Miller over here, Ryan," Benson said.

"Sergeant," Ryan began, turning to Clemmens, "could you keep the bodies here for, say, ten minutes?"

"No, he can't!"

All three men turned quickly and faced Lieutenant Stein. The large man was standing with his back to the sun. His face was completely shadowed. "Let's clear this area, Clemmens, and get this fucking investigation underway!"

The man's voice was shaking. Benson heard the fear and the horror in it. He wondered if Stein was that inexperienced or if he was getting old.

Clemmens shook his head at Ryan. "We'll take 'em all down to the morgue. I'll wait there till you bring your man."

"Thanks, Clemmens," Ryan said.

Ryan called Miller, and the contact agreed to meet the detectives at the county morgue. When Ryan returned to Benson, the two men began walking through the warehouse looking for something that might truly link Kenyatta with the massacre. But all they found was the ever-present shadow of Lieutenant Stein, who followed them step for step.

Johnny Miller arrived at the county coroner's office a half hour after Ryan had made the call. The thin black man was dressed up as usual, but his mannerisms were shaky and nervous. Benson and Ryan greeted him outside the morgue itself.

"What's up?" Miller asked, trying to sound light.

"It's these dead men, Johnny. We figured you might be able to identify a few," Benson replied.

"Oh, man, what a drag!" Miller followed the two detectives into the morgue room, where they were greeted by a small white man wearing a smock. In the corner of the room, Lieutenant Stein leaned against the wall watching the trio very carefully.

The attendant pulled out the six drawers with the sheet-covered bodies lying side by side on slabs. Benson and Ryan stood behind Miller as he walked along the row looking down at each face. Finally, he came to the end and turned to Benson.

"Wilbur Chamus. They're his dudes."

"You sure of that?" Benson asked.

"No doubt, man. Those cats had it wired down there in Watts. Seen them all over the fuckin' place!"

Benson smiled to himself. With the discovery of the strongbox and now the massacre, the operation was coming together. The links between Chamus and Kenyatta were being made. The only problem now was to find out why it had happened, why the men had clashed at the warehouse.

"Johnny," Benson began after a moment, "who's the dude who laid it down to you about the big shipment?"

Miller frowned, then turned his back to the corpses lying on the slabs. "Man, I don't know…."

"Listen, Johnny, we got to know," Benson urged.

"Okay, but let me outta this shit. I tell you the dude's name and you forget it, you dig where I'm comin' from? I mean, too many dudes been dyin' 'round here!"

"All right, Miller. Tell us the name and we'll call it even."

Miller looked from Benson to Ryan and then quickly at Stein. "His name's Horning. Small, fat dude…, black. Haven't seen him since that night he laid down the shit to me."

The name did not ring a bell; neither man had heard it before. When Benson turned to ask Stein if he had ever heard the name, he discovered the lieutenant had left the room.

"Shit, man," Miller said quickly. "Get me a fuckin' ticket outta this town! There's some heavy shit goin' down. Real heavy!"

Benson looked quickly at Ryan, and the two men communicated in silence. Finally, Ryan fished out a hundred-dollar bill and put it into Miller's hand. He told the man to be careful and led him to the door. After Miller had gone, he returned to Benson.

"Where'd Stein go?" Ryan asked.

"Damned if I know. But I'll tell you one thing. This thing is big. Bigger than anything Kenyatta's gotten himself into before."

"No doubt, Ben," Ryan replied. "But where do we go now?"

Benson led the way out of the sterile room, thanked the attendant, then turned to Ryan after they were outside in the hallway. "We got to find Horning. He's our main man right now. We'll call Comstock and see if the Feds have anything on him, all right?"

Ryan nodded. "Yeah, but I have a feeling we better move fast. This thing looks like it's going to blow."

"Man," Benson chuckled sardonically, "with Kenyatta, the fuse is always lit!"

10

ONCE AGAIN, THE ELITE of Kenyatta's group were gathered in the black leader's apartment. Duke Simms, Amos Cortner, Mike Allen, and Stonewall Manfred sat on the large couch sipping their drinks quietly. Elliot Stone and Kenyatta stood at the bar, with Rufus and Edgar seated on dining-room chairs against the wall. In the center of the room was Wilbur Chamus, a shaken and broken man who was bartering for his life.

For over ten hours Kenyatta had been with the man attempting to break him down. It had taken a little heavy-handed work to convince the former kingpin that his glory days were over. But after a few raps against the side of the face, struck by Elliot Stone in such a manner as to leave no traces, Chamus had finally agreed to call his man outside the city.

The phone call had been made, and Chamus had told his connect that he had a source of heroin unequaled in the country. The connect had taken Chamus' phone number and told him to wait for his return call. That had been two hours ago, and the men had waited during that time for the response.

"Now remember, Chamus," Kenyatta said coldly, "when he calls, you tell him like I told you."

Chamus nodded. "Yeah," he began, his voice weak with terror and fatigue. "You won't deal with anyone but the big man. I'll tell him."

"You'd better, my man," Kenyatta said. "Or else your fuckin' life ain't worth a piece of shit! You dig where I'm comin' from?"

"Yeah. Yeah, I dig it." Chamus stared straight ahead, his eyes following the pattern on the rug in small circles. He had been confronted with that onslaught of Kenyatta throughout the long and bloody day.

At ten minutes to nine, the phone rang. Kenyatta picked up the receiver and handed it to Chamus. The look in the black man's eyes was enough to frighten any man. It practically turned Chamus speechless.

Wilbur Chamus spoke for ten minutes, mostly nodding his head and answering with short "yeahs." The conversation finished, he hung up the phone and turned to Kenyatta.

"He'll meet us," Chamus said softly.

"Where?" Kenyatta asked quickly.

"In the desert, out of town. Near Barstow."

At least, Kenyatta thought, they were moving out of the ghetto and closer to some of the big action. Barstow could mean only one thing—Las Vegas. And coming out of that town meant the organization, the brotherhood, the Mafia, or whatever one chose to call it. "Okay, when is it set?"

Chamus asked for a cigarette before replying. "Tomorrow night. Nine o'clock. The old Hanson Ranch, just outside of town."

"Will he be alone?" Stone asked, speaking for the first time.

Chamus looked warily at the man he had ordered killed. The sight of Elliot Stone still alive had sent cold chills down the man's spine. It was an omen, an indication to Chamus that his end had come. He knew now that he would be fortunate just to survive what lay ahead.

"I said, my man," Stone exclaimed, "will he be alone?"

Chamus nodded. "He knows the stuff's all right, 'cause I told him it was. He wants you to bring it yourself…, all of it."

Kenyatta chuckled. "Sure, man. Now, why don't you go into the other apartment with Rufus and Edgar here and get yourself some sleep."

Chamus struggled to his feet, with Edgar and Rufus on either side. Each man grabbed an arm and led Chamus from the living room. Kenyatta called out to his two men and tossed them a fifth of Jack Daniels.

Rufus caught the bottle and grinned back at his man. "Thanks, my man. Goin' be a long fuckin' night!"

Kenyatta walked around behind the bar and rested his elbows on the fine mahogany. "Well, I don't rightly know. I'm goin' out there tomorrow night, with Elliot here right beside me and a backup car on the road. Aside from that, I can't tell nothin' till we know who it is that we're meetin' with."

"I can dig that, Ken," Stonewall said. "But we're gettin' pretty fuckin' close to the main supplier, ain't we? I mean, shouldn't we lay down some kind of precautions?"

Kenyatta stroked his bald pate for a moment before replying. "You're right, my man. I was thinkin' that each of you get your people together and prepare them for travelin'. Get your cars filled with gas, get your rods together…, all the shit you'll need."

"Is that it, man?" Simms asked.

"Yeah, just be ready for a phone call from me. I'll call you dudes at Stonewall's place."

"Where do you think it'll be comin' down, Ken?" Simms asked.

Kenyatta took a long sip from his drink, then placed the glass gently on the counter. He looked to Stone. "Where do you think, Elliot?"

Stone did not hesitate. "Las Vegas. The way things are lookin'. The man's bringin' the stuff in by car. It's the dude we saw those times out front of Chamus' place. No doubt that the pickup was close by. Now, with the desert scene happenin' out there in Barstow, I would lay odds it was Vegas."

"That's about the way I see it, too," Kenyatta added. "An' that's where I hope we finally get. I mean, if this dude's willin' to come out all the way to Barstow, then we'll hit him there if we can. If not, we'll get him in Vegas. But we got to be sure first."

The four men on the couch stood up and made ready to depart. "Listen, Kenyatta," Simms said, "if you need a goddamn army, we'll have one waitin' for you. You dig?"

Kenyatta smiled and grasped Simms' hand. "Yeah, dude, I dig where you're comin' from. Let's get it movin'. You're gonna hear from me tomorrow night."

The men shook hands all around, and finally only Stone and Kenyatta were left in the living room. Kenyatta poured another round of drinks and the two men drank in silence.

"You know somethin', Elliot," Kenyatta began after refilling the glasses. "After all the shit I been through, I begin to think that finally it's goin' to pay off."

"I see where you're comin' from," Stone replied.

"Yeah," Kenyatta continued, his voice softer now. "There was nothin' as big as this shit goin' down in Detroit. I mean, seemed like all we hassled with were a bunch of street pushers and fucked-up junkies. But this scene, well, this is somethin' different."

Stone nodded. "You think we'll be able to pull it off?"

"Shit, man!" Kenyatta exclaimed. "Man like me waits all his fuckin' life to pull somethin' like this off, and he knows he's got to. Ain't no two ways 'bout it, my man!"

Stone laughed and Kenyatta joined him. Both men knew within twenty-four hours they were going up against men who would just as soon kill a man as look at him. They also knew they were going up against men, possibly white men, who had the law on their side. They were the controlling powers, the fat honkies who sat back in their leather office chairs dealing out death and corruption with one flick of their pudgy pink fingers. These were the men whom Kenyatta had always been after, yet men whom he had never really seen. The possibility that finally he would be meeting them face to face was an invigorating thought.

Kenyatta and Stone drank in silence. Both men thought about the events of that day and what would be the events of the upcoming days. In their own separate ways, they were both grateful that Chamus had hit the O.E.O. house when he had.

Finally, Kenyatta put his drink down and stood erect. "Man, I got me a beautiful woman waiting in the bedroom there."

"Ain't no better way to relieve tension, Ken," Stone said with a grin, realizing how much he himself needed a woman right then.

Kenyatta smiled. "I'll see you later, my man. You just make yourself comfortable, dig?"

Elliot Stone nodded and watched Kenyatta as the big man strode across the living room and into the bedroom.

The room was dark, but the outline of Betty's naked

figure beneath the sheets was visible as some light poured in through the window outside. Kenyatta stood above the bed and stared down at her brown flesh, her slightly parted lips, and her smooth, high forehead.

"Hey, you awake?" he asked in a whisper.

Betty stretched out, pulling her arms above her head. The sheet fell below her large, moon-shaped breasts revealing her silver-dollar nipples. As she opened her eyes and saw Kenyatta getting undressed above her, her nipples began to pucker. Soon, the tips were erect.

"Baby...," Kenyatta said as he crawled into bed next to his woman. Betty stretched her long, lean legs out and threw one over Kenyatta's hip. Seductively, she pushed her moist sex against him.

Kenyatta smiled and pulled the woman to him. He drew her mouth against his, and their tongues clashed in a practiced rhythm of moist contact.

"Oh, baby!" Kenyatta moaned as he rolled over and lifted himself between her widespread legs. Betty raised her hips off the bed, then reached down and took her man's throbbing sex and guided him into her moist valley.

"Take me, Ken! Please!" Betty cried as Kenyatta drove smoothly and gently into her depths.

Kenyatta lit a cigarette for both of them after they had finished. He felt deliciously drained, as though all the tension and fatigue of the day had been sucked out of him in one beautiful surge. Betty lay on her back next to him, still trembling from her climax.

"Ken?" Betty began softly.

"Yeah, babe...?"

"I'm frightened, Ken. I'm scared about what's happening with Chamus."

Kenyatta chuckled. She had been through some horrible things with him, and every time she had voiced the same kind of fear. Yes, Kenyatta thought, I would have been worried if she hadn't said anything.

"I mean it, Ken," Betty insisted. "I'm frightened of this whole thing. I mean, you don't really know what you're getting into, do you?"

"Listen, honey," Kenyatta replied. "I've gone into things before that I didn't know about. This ain't nothin' new. And besides, it's worth it, ain't it?"

"Yes, I suppose." Betty fell into a deep silence. They lay in bed smoking cigarettes, with the only sound being that of their breath as they exhaled. After a while, Kenyatta felt the bed shaking slightly and he knew that Betty was crying. He reached across to her and took her hand and held it against his chest. They slept like that until morning, when Stone knocked loudly on the door to awaken them.

At ten o'clock in the morning, after a huge breakfast fixed by Betty, Kenyatta was ready to leave. He, Stone, and Chamus would ride in the Cadillac, with Rufus and Edgar trailing behind in a Chevrolet.

Elliot Stone sat on the couch cleaning his .45 and checking the trigger action. Chamus, having been brought into the room by Edgar and Rufus, sat in the same chair in the center of the room. His hands were tied behind his back. He sported a new suit and otherwise looked like the Chamus of old.

Kenyatta entered the room wearing a leather jacket and a tight-fitting turtleneck. He glanced about, patted the inside of his coat to make sure the .38 was in place, and then walked over to where Chamus was sitting.

"You ready to meet your goddamn white motherfuckin' friends, Chamus?"

Wilbur Chamus sat with head down on a chair. What had once been a totally arrogant stature had degenerated into a humble, almost pathetic stance.

Kenyatta grabbed the lapel of Chamus' coat and hoisted the man to his feat. "Okay, dude, you're ridin' with us." Then, turning to Rufus, he asked, "Got the wheels ready?"

"Both are waitin' downstairs, Ken," Rufus replied.

"All right, then, let's split," Kenyatta led the way, pushing Chamus in front of him while Rufus, Edgar, and Elliot followed behind.

The street was empty for a Friday morning. A few cars glided by, but the usual business traffic was not present. The Cadillac and the green Chevrolet waited, parked next to each other. Kenyatta went straight to the Caddy, opened the rear door, and shoved Chamus inside.

"Okay," he said to Rufus and Edgar. "We get split up, meet us at the Denny's in Barstow."

The two men nodded and climbed into the Chevrolet.

Elliot Stone got behind the steering wheel, checked

the automatic locks on the doors in the rear, then started up the car. Kenyatta climbed in next to him, pulled out his .38, and laid the pistol down on the seat between them. "Just in case our nigger friend back there tries anythin'," he said.

Stone smiled back, then pulled away from the curb.

They took the freeways out of Los Angeles through the San Fernando Valley and out into the San Gabriel Mountains. In another hour they passed through Lancaster, the first town in the Mojave Desert, and followed the freeway toward the town of Mojave.

The heroin had been stashed in the lining of the ceiling, in case they were stopped by the highway patrol. Nevertheless, Kenyatta began to grow uptight about Stone's excessive speed. "Hey, man, just cool it. I'm gettin' a fuckin' jet lag!"

Stone laughed and eased up on the accelerator. It felt good to be driving the powerful car out in the open expanse of the desert. The air was clear, no smog, and the sun was bright and direct. The highway was flat and built for speed.

Rufus and Edgar followed close behind in the green Chevrolet, keeping pace with the Cadillac. Each time Stone looked into the rearview mirror, he could see the two men speaking animatedly with each other, gesturing and laughing.

They passed Boron, a mining town, and headed into the last stretch of desert before Barstow. Since leaving Los Angeles, Chamus had not spoken a word. He had sat in his seat with his head bent forward. Finally, Kenyatta became upset with the man's silence.

"Hey, man," he began harshly, "you better start talkin' a little 'fore you forget how!"

Chamus glanced up, nodding as though coming out of a stupor. He stared blankly at Kenyatta.

"Tell me you're doin' fine, nigger!" Kenyatta ordered, lifting the pistol above the seat so that Chamus could see it.

"I'm...doin'...fine...," Chamus mumbled.

"That's better, fucker!" Kenyatta said, then turned back to watch the road ahead.

Stone glanced at the big black man next to him and felt a tinge of worry creep through his gut. He had never known Kenyatta to be so edgy, so willing to put a man down like he had just done with Chamus. He wondered if, for the first time in his life, Kenyatta was actually afraid.

"You okay?" Stone asked.

Kenyatta nodded. "Sure, man, no reason not to be."

But there was still something in Kenyatta's voice that Stone did not like, a tone that did not express the strength and courage the man usually had.

When the small caravan reached Barstow, Chamus directed Stone toward the outskirts of town. They passed through the small city, then turned onto a two-lane road heading north into the desert. Within five minutes, they were out in the middle of nowhere. They drove for another five miles before reaching an old battered sign that read "Hanson Ranch."

"That's it," Kenyatta said, pointing out the sign.

"Yup," Chamus said.

"It is fucking desolate out here!" Kenyatta exclaimed as Stone slowed down the car and pulled to the side of the road.

"Is this where we're meetin' tonight?" Stone asked.

Chamus nodded. "Five hundred yards after the sign..., that's what he said."

Rufus and Edgar pulled up behind the Cadillac and stopped. Both men hopped out of the car and came up on either side.

"This is it," Stone said to Rufus.

Rufus looked around at the desolation and frowned. Up ahead there was a small rise in the road, but other than that everything was flat and empty. "Man, this is some perfect place for birddoggin'."

"No shit," Stone agreed. "Talk about your wide-open spaces!"

Kenyatta had gotten out of the car and was scanning the area. Finally he moved to the front of the car and spoke to Rufus and Edgar. "Tonight I want you dudes up on the hill, you dig where I'm comin' from?"

"Yeah," Rufus answered for both of them.

"An' I want you facing down this way, ready to flash your lights on if we need it. Up there you'll be able to hear and see everythin' that's comin' down. Dig?"

Rufus and Edgar both nodded. In the backseat of their car were two shotguns, two high-powered rifles, and three .38 pistols. They were ready for whatever might come down that night.

"Okay," Kenyatta said finally. "Let's move back to town and get something to eat."

The Motel 6 in Barstow was a large, rectangular building with half the rooms facing a parking lot in the rear. Stone had rented one of these rooms, and the rest of the group were able to climb the stairs and enter it without being seen. Inside the small cubicle, the entourage lounged away the afternoon, eating the fried chicken they had ordered and watching television.

Each man, silent in his own thoughts, was preparing himself for what the night might bring. The only exception was Wilbur Chamus who knew deep down inside that, no matter what he did, he would soon be a dead man. His desperate thinking, his ordeal of attempting to discover a way out, had left him drained and exhausted. He slept soundly throughout the afternoon on the small lounge chair in the motel room.

Over one hundred and fifty miles northeast of Barstow, Clement Jenkins stood on the twentieth floor of the Sands Hotel. The white-haired man, now in his late sixties, gazed out the huge picture window of his penthouse suite. Beneath him were the buildings, the casinos, the hotels, and the multitudes of people swarming the Las Vegas Strip. Beyond them was the clear, distant desert.

"Well?" Oscar Manning asked.

Jenkins turned slowly to his prime heroin runner and stroked his small mustache thoughtfully. "Oscar, I think we should take a stab. The man is obviously intent on moving his stuff, and if he's black, he's going to sell at a very low price."

Oscar Manning, a white man in his early fifties, a former real-estate broker who had finally discovered where the big money was, just nodded. He had come a long way in his fifty years but nothing compared to Clement Jenkins.

Clement Jenkins had inherited over half a million dollars and a small light-bulb factory from his father. Jenkins had been twenty-nine at the time and broke. With his gift he began manufacturing Christmas tree lights, then outdoor lights, and finally cornered the market on fluorescent lights. After that, it was all gravy.

But Clement Jenkins was one of those men to whom wealth was immaterial. It was the making of the money that counted, the continual process of gaining more and more, stockpiling it until there was nothing left to do but count it. Thus, Jenkins had begun importing rare and exotic narcotics.

Twenty years ago he had begun with hashish. During the fifties he had graduated to cocaine. When the sixties arrived, he had financed a young chemist in San Francisco to produce huge amounts of LSD. Then, finally, Clement Jenkins had begun selling, importing, and dealing in heroin. Of course, one of Jenkins' motivations for this line of business was personal. Clement Jenkins had been a heroin addict for the past ten years.

But sitting atop the Sands in his privately owned suite, Clement Jenkins was considered by everyone to be the most upright, honorable citizen in Las Vegas. He supplied jobs for thousands of people with his casi nos and nightclubs, and his effect on local politics was powerful and certain.

For Oscar Manning, Clement Jenkins was the top man. A man who made it himself. Thus, it was with hesitation that Manning asked his boss the next question.

"Are you sure it's worth dealing with a black?"

Jenkins looked at Manning, then sat down slowly in his leather chair. "Oscar, there are some things better left to certain people. The French and Italians for many years have been supplying us with top-grade stuff. But the political pressures raise the prices, and the smugglers hesitate to take the chances without sufficient compensation. With blacks, it's different. They'll take the chances because they don't have a future anyway. They dislike themselves so much, through conditioning, that they'll submit to the most ludicrous deals. In other words, Oscar, they are the easiest race of people in the world to give the shaft to."

Manning laughed. "Yeah, Clement, I can see your point."

"Yes, Oscar," Jenkins mused, "I think we will deal with this man. After all, a pound of heroin is a pound of heroin, and a black is a black."

Manning watched his man as he spun around in his chair and returned to his panoramic view of the desert town of Las Vegas.

At precisely nine o'clock that night, Oscar Manning, along with two armed bodyguards, pulled to a stop on the Hanson Road five hundred yards beyond the sign. The night was bright around them. The stars glistened and the desert was quiet.

Five minutes later, Kenyatta's Cadillac pulled up alongside Manning's limousine. Chamus climbed out of the backseat, and Kenyatta emerged from the front.

Manning climbed out of the back of the limousine and confronted both Kenyatta and Chamus in the small space between the cars. The huge size of the bald-headed black man shook Manning, and he found himself backing away even before the men began speaking.

"It's all right, man," Chamus said, his voice shaky and uncertain.

"Listen, man," Kenyatta said quickly, "I'm here to deal. That's all."

Manning looked past Kenyatta and into the Cadillac. All he saw was Elliot Stone. He looked fairly harmless. "Okay," Manning said. "Talk."

"You know what's happening, man. You know what I got. I want the bread in cash. Half deposited at a bank in Algiers, half in cash. Payment upon delivery, you dig?"

"Yes, I understand," Manning replied. "Seven hundred thousand?"

"Eight," Kenyatta replied quickly.

"Seven seventy-five. That's a limit."

The men stood in silence for a moment. Kenyatta shrugged his shoulders. "Just a minute, man. I got to speak with my partner."

Kenyatta turned away from the men and leaned into

the car. He knew it was safe because Rufus and Edgar had their high-powered rifles trained on the two men. Chamus would not dare to make a move.

"What you think, Elliot?" Kenyatta asked.

Stone leaned across the seat so that he could be heard. In a whisper he said, "The dude is Oscar Manning, the runner. We had the motherfucker in the pictures, Kenyatta."

Kenyatta smiled at Stone. "Thanks, man."

Chamus and Manning waited between the cars, with Manning attempting to make pleasant conversation with the former big wheel from Watts. Kenyatta stepped between the two men and spoke to them both at the same time.

"I dug it," Kenyatta began in his coldest voice, "that you were taking me to the fuckin' top, Chamus. An' not to some white honkie runner. You dig where I'm comin' from?"

Manning could feel the cold sweat forming quickly on his body as Kenyatta spoke. As a reflexive action, he turned back to the men sitting in his car. Kenyatta grabbed the white man's shoulder and spun him around. "I wouldn't do that, man," Kenyatta warned. "I got two high-powered motherfuckers sittin' on that hill up there ready to blow your motherfuckin' brains out!"

"Okay," Manning begged. "Please...."

Kenyatta laughed sardonically, then released his grip. "Okay then," he began. "You take me to the man. The man and no one else, an' I'll deal."

"But we never...," Manning began.

"You never what? Bullshit! This is a new day, Jack, and if you want what I got, we deal with the man. You dig?"

Manning shrugged. "I'll call him."

"You do that!" Kenyatta shouted.

Manning got into the backseat of his limousine and picked up the phone. He explained the situation. Then he listened. Finally, he hung up the phone.

"He wants to see me before he deals with you," Manning explained weakly.

Kenyatta thought quickly. He could keep Manning under the barrel of his gun, but that would set off the big man. The closest he would ever get to the source would then be one of his flunkies. He would have to take the chance with Manning and hope that the man was as greedy as he thought he was. It was his only chance to get to the top.

"Okay. Give me a number to call."

Manning reached into his pocket and pulled out a card. Kenyatta took the card and guessed at the prefix on the phone number. "Vegas, eh?"

Manning nodded. "That's right. Call him tonight."

Kenyatta nodded. Manning got into the backseat of the car and told his driver to take him back. All the while, Chamus was trying to tell Manning something, staring at him intently with begging eyes. But in the darkness of the desert night, the black man's attempt failed.

"In the car, Chamus!" Kenyatta ordered. Chamus jumped into the backseat and Kenyatta got into the front. "Drive, Elliot. We got to get to a phone booth.

Stonewall and the others shouldn't be more than two hours behind us if we get them drivin' right now."

Elliot Stone flashed his headlights twice to signal Rufus and Edgar, then spun the car around and headed back to Barstow. His adrenaline was flowing like crazy. This time around, he could sense that they were really onto something worthwhile. "Man," he exclaimed to Kenyatta, "I'm beginning to enjoy this shit!"

"I can dig it," Kenyatta replied softly. "I can dig it!"

AT ABOUT THE TIME Kenyatta and his men were heading into Las Vegas, Johnny Miller was packing furiously. In his small bachelor apartment on Adams Boulevard, the slightly-built Negro was putting together his bare essentials. His closet was full of fine threads, but Miller had suddenly lost his interest in clothes.

The events of the day had confirmed in his mind the need to get out of town, and to get out fast. He had known since that first day when Benson and Ryan had approached that something big was coming down. But the money and the protection that the two detectives offered him were enough to allay his fears. Not so anymore. Not with those six corpses lying motion-less and twisted in the morgue.

Miller tightened the last strap on his bag and took another long swig on his bottle. The effect of the booze was getting to him, allowing him to relax and feel mellow. But even though his body was easing off, his mind was screaming at him. Warning him to get out.

The knock on the door came abruptly and without the usual warning of approaching footsteps. Miller spun on his heels and faced the door. "Yeah?" he shouted without thinking.

"Miller? Johnny Miller?" the voice called out.

"Who's there?" Miller asked.

"Stein. Lieutenant Stein. I was with Benson and Ryan earlier. I just wanted you to confirm one pho-tograph."

Miller breathed much easier now. He recognized the man's voice and knew it to be Stein. Quickly, he opened the door and stood aside as Lieutenant Stein pushed his heavy frame into the apartment.

"How'd you find me, man?" Miller asked.

"Benson. He gave me your address," Stein replied, surveying the room, his eyes finally coming to rest on the suitcase lying on the bed. "You leaving, eh?"

"Yeah, daddy," Miller replied quickly. "Things get-tin' to be just a little hot out west."

Stein smoothed down his thinning hair and smiled. "Probably a good idea, after what happened today. You know?"

"I can dig it, man. Now, if you'll just get on with

it, I can get myself groovin'."

Stein reached inside his coat pocket. Miller watched him closely. Suddenly, the slim black man was standing face to face with a police special. The gleaming barrel of the pistol was pointed directly at Miller's forehead.

"Hey, man," Miller exclaimed. "What is this shit?"

"You little nigger," Stein said coldly. "You fuckin' little nigger. Playing both sides against the middle. You should have known one day it would close in on you."

Miller stared into Stein's pale eyes and saw nothing. He knew the man meant to kill him, and there would be no way to talk him out of it.

"Please, man," Miller begged, his voice cracking, "I ain't done nothin' no sensible nigger wouldn't have done. You know that!"

Stein just laughed as he pulled out a silencer and began screwing the pipe onto the barrel. "You little niggers are all alike. You think you're in the big time. You do nothing but fuck it up for everyone else!"

Johnny Miller lost his ability to speak as Lieutenant Stein raised his pistol toward the black man's face. Stein closed his eyes as he pulled the trigger.

The bullet penetrated Miller's forehead just above the bridge of his nose. A tiny hole appeared where the bullet had made entry, and a stream of blood began pouring out of the hole. The bullet had entered Miller so cleanly that the black man was not thrown back by the impact. Instead, he stood weaving in his place, his eyes still open with the look of horror that had invaded them when Stein had raised his pistol.

The large lieutenant looked at his victim for a moment, then reached out and pushed Miller backward. The slightly-built black man fell in a heap on the floor, his eyes still open and his wound still bleeding.

Quickly Stein packed his weapon and left. He locked the door behind him. He figured it would be days before anyone would find the body.

The Paradise Room on Manchester Boulevard was Stein's next stop. It was a large room, usually filled with hundreds of jazz aficionados. Tonight, Gloria Lynn was appearing with Harry "Sweets" Edison. Stein pulled into the crowded parking lot of the nightclub and walked across the pavement toward the entrance.

The black man standing at the door looked down at the police badge that Stein produced and nodded for him to pass by.

The club was dark and smoke-filled. The tables were packed with people, all of them black, listening to the tender voice of Miss Lynn as she moved gracefully through "On Green Dolphin Street."

Stein moved through the back of the club along the wall until he reached the bar. The long wooden surface was filled with drinks and ashtrays. Each stool was occupied as a few hookers and a lot of men listened to the song. Stein walked slowly along the bar until he reached the second to the last stool and found what he was looking for. "Horning?" he said directly to the plump, balding Negro sitting on the stool.

Horning looked up at the white face of Stein and knew instantly that he was police. Only the white cops dared to come into the all-black nightclub. And that was because they carried guns.

"Horning, come with me." Stein produced his badge again and showed it quickly to the small black man.

Horning looked around him quickly. He was trapped. If he made a scene in the club, his reputation as a street man and reliable contact would be blown. And if he was seen walking out with Stein, he would be fingered as a pigeon. A lot of the tougher dudes in the club were already watching the silent confrontation at the bar, a lot of men whom Horning relied upon for his business.

"Worried about your friends, are you?" Stein asked.

Horning nodded.

Stein grinned, reached out, and took Horning's arm. He led the man through the darkened nightclub quickly, sometimes giving the small black man a convincing nudge. After they were outside, Stein pushed Horning across the parking lot and into his car. Then Stein jumped behind the wheel and drove off, heading down Manchester Boulevard toward the ocean.

"What's this all about, man?" Horning asked, his voice high-pitched and tinged with fear.

"You should know," Stein replied simply.

"Man, I don't. You dig?"

Stein chuckled. "You set it up, right? A bum setup with a dangerous man. Lots of deaths. All kinds of shit."

Horning felt himself sink. After setting up the initial meeting, he had thought himself out in the clear. No more hassles, just sit back and wait for the money to be dumped into his lap. Complications were something that the small, rotund black man did not consider. But now, he wished he had.

Stein began humming a tune as he drove farther out toward the ocean. He took Horning through Hermosa Beach, then turned left on the Pacific Coast Highway and headed toward the gigantic oil refinery in the distance.

"A pretty sight, eh?" Stein asked jovially, as if the two men were on a sightseeing trip.

Horning looked at the massive structure, the lit beams of steel, and the huge smokestacks. The prettiest sight the man could hope to see now would be his own life, secure and with a future.

Stein drove the car toward the huge refinery, then pulled off the road on a desolate section of the beach. He stopped the car and turned to Horning. "Okay, nigger," he said, "this is where you get off."

Horning stared back at the heavyset lieutenant. He was screaming a thousand words inside. His skull was crying out with pleas for his life. But as much as he tried, he could not utter them. His mouth just opened and closed in silence.

"Go ahead, Horning," Stein ordered. It was as simple as that. Horning knew what was coming, yet he was powerless to stop himself as he reached for the door handle and yanked it up. He felt the cool night air of the ocean and he could hear the sounds of the waves crashing nearby.

As he stared at Stein, the lieutenant was screwing his silencer onto the barrel of his pistol. Now, whatever doubt or hope Horning might have had was gone. Still, he moved as if in a dream, climbing quietly out of the car.

He stood next to the open car door peering in at his slayer. Lieutenant Stein held the pistol with two hands, as he had been taught in the academy, and pulled the trigger.

The bullet struck Horning in the neck. His cords and muscles seemed to explode from that area. Red seeped down across his upper chest, and the black man fell backward onto the sand.

Stein put his pistol back into his shoulder holster after removing the silencer. He leaned across the seat, groaning loudly with the strain of the movement, and pulled the door closed. As he backed up, his headlights drifted across the still twitching body of Horning. The black man was crying, and uttering guttural sounds that drifted with the wind. Stein smiled to himself and drove back onto the Pacific Coast Highway toward the airport.

His job was finished and Stein felt an incredible sense of relief flood his mind. He had taken the orders from his man, the go-ahead to eliminate the two blacks who had set Chamus up with Kenyatta. After those were carried out, Stein would then take his long trip to Mexico. Upon his return, the whole situation that had blown way out of proportion in the Los Angeles ghetto would be solved.

The turnoff to the Los Angeles International Airport was empty. For a Friday night, it was an odd state of affairs but Stein welcomed it. He drove quickly down Century Boulevard and into the circle roadway that would carry him to his terminal. He turned into a parking lot opposite the Mexicana Airlines terminal and parked. His luggage was in the trunk; hurriedly Stein pulled it out.

Just as the police lieutenant was about to slam the trunk door, he heard footsteps behind him. Two men were approaching quickly, the intent in their walk unmistakable.

Stein whirled on his heels just in time to see one of the men raising a sawed-off shotgun toward his head. The huge explosion was muffled in the heavy sea air, and the second round seemed even less noticeable.

Stein did not have time to react. The first shell hit him directly in the face, ripping away the flesh around his mouth and cheeks. The entire lower part of his face became a seething mass of blood and bone tissue. The second shell hit just a little lower, around the neck. Basically, it took the man's head off, leaving only one muscle cord to keep the large head attached to the body.

A second after the two blasts from the shotgun, a 747 jetliner took off. The thundering roar of the plane's engines covered any trace of what had happened.

Lieutenant Stein's mutilated body was the first of the three to be discovered. An elderly couple returning from the terminal after seeing their children off to their home in the East stumbled onto the remains of the police officer. While trying to comfort his fainting wife, the old man called the police.

The word of Stein's death spread quickly through the Los Angeles police building. It was quickly picked up by Detectives Ryan and Benson as they were leaving headquarters. The two officers raced across town on the crowded freeways toward the airport.

When they arrived at the parking lot, the scene of the killing was cordoned off by uniformed police and airport security. FBI Agent Comstock was standing just outside the small circle of men when Benson and Ryan managed to push their way through the crowd of the morbidly curious.

"It looked like a hit," Comstock said as he led Benson and Ryan to where the body lay.

Stein's fleshy figure was plastered against the open trunk of his car. Half of his head had been shot off. Blood, excrement, and urine covered his frame in equal parts.

"Jesus," Ryan exclaimed when he saw the body. "They weren't fooling, were they?"

"You find anything else?" Benson asked Comstock.

The tall black agent turned to the black officer and frowned. "In the file we found...the inside man at the department?"

Benson nodded. He had suspected it all along.

"Well," Comstock continued, "this was our baby. His bags were packed and he had a passport and a visa to Mexico. Also, his pistol had been fired four times within the last two, maybe three hours."

Benson turned to Ryan. "We got an address on Johnny Miller?" he asked.

Ryan nodded. "Yeah, we got an address."

Benson explained the situation to Comstock and what his theory was. "Basically," the black detective said, "the bastards are cleaning their house. They're hitting everyone who could place the ring in jeopardy."

"And if we don't get there before the fuckers are all massacred, we lose, right?" Comstock tensed.

Benson stared at the ground. "That's right, Comstock. It's coming down fast, and we're still a couple of steps behind."

Benson and Ryan left Comstock with the body of what once had been a policeman, a respected man of the community. Later, they would dig through the various bank accounts and investments of Lieutenant Stein and discover the man was worth more than two hundred thousand dollars. None of that had come from the man's modest salary.

The two Detroit detectives drove across town. The night was brightly lit throughout Los Angeles, and wherever they stopped they saw couples and single people gathered in their cars having a good Friday night. Benson looked out the windows at these people and wondered.

They had been stalking the trail of death for the last couple of weeks. Men were dying, men who were virtual unknowns outside the cloudy arena of crime in which they lived. Benson wondered if those men who dealt in death had ever taken their pleasures on a warm Friday night like the people he was seeing this night.

The modern apartment house on Adams was still noisy with sounds of a Friday night party. People were laughing, unaware that within a few feet a man lay murdered.

Benson and Ryan pulled their guns out of their coats and walked carefully through the patio. Ryan led the way, taking the steps slowly up to the second floor. At the end of the balcony was the well-lit apartment. Both men stopped and looked through the window at the people inside.

For a moment, Benson hoped that Miller was all right. Had he been shot, he figured, the people in the apartment nearby would have heard the report.

But when Ryan opened the door, using a small pass key, Benson's hopes for Johnny Miller dissolved quickly.

The slightly-built black man lay sprawled on the floor. His body was riddled with the results of the gunshot. The small hole in the man's forehead had coagulated and remained just a tiny, crusty brown spot.

"Another hit," Ryan said softly, leaning down over the body of Miller.

"Looked like he was leaving, too," Benson said, picking up the man's traveling bag. "Man, the dude sure dug his clothes!"

The closet was still full of Miller's threads. Benson looked at the patterns and the colors, remembering how the little hustler had been wary of taking on the role as an informer. The feelings toward what was coming down in Los Angeles had been too rampant at that time. Even little Johnny Miller had felt the tension—the aura of violence that had been building.

The two detectives called the coroner and the investigating officer. Lab tests would be made on the slugs taken from Miller's body, and they would match those fired from Stein's gun. Benson and Ryan would remember the scene in the county morgue the day they brought in the four bodies from the warehouse massacre. They would remember Miller identifying the corpses, and Stein leaning against the wall listening.

It was an hour after the discovery of Miller's body that Benson and Ryan received the call that Horning's body had been found on a beach in Santa Monica. The detectives drove back across town and examined the remains of the round, balding black man.

Benson and Ryan stood in silence looking down on the dead man as the wind blew in off the Pacific Ocean. Inside, the two men were feeling the same frustration and rage. It wasn't the fact that these two men had been killed. It was more that they were always cleaning up after the slayers, following them through a trail of mutilated corpses, whether they were the victim of an overdose or the recipient of a bullet.

"Goddamn!" Benson exclaimed as he climbed into the car with his partner. "I've seen some fucking vendettas in my time, but nothing like this."

"Yeah," Ryan agreed. "Wherever Kenyatta is and whatever he's doing, he's dealing with some big motherfuckers!"

Benson leaned back in his seat and lit a cigarette. His mind traveled back to his warm house in Detroit. He hadn't seen his wife in some time. He missed her warm, brown skin, her gentle and easy manner in bed. But most of all, he missed dealing with a human being, a woman who was not involved in the bloodshed and insanity that had been his life for too long now.

"Man," Benson said as Ryan pulled out onto the Pacific Coast Highway, "I got to get home."

"I know what you mean, partner," Ryan replied. "And I have a feeling it isn't going to be too long."

"Everybody's dying, pal. And all we do is go around and pick up the bodies."

Ryan chuckled, a sardonic, almost wicked laugh. "That's what we're paid to do, Ben. Nothing more, nothing less."

Benson sighed. "There's got to be more," he said quietly.

Ryan looked at his partner and smiled. "Don't bet on it, Ben," he said.

The two men drove off into the Los Angeles night, no closer to finding the elusive Kenyatta than they had been when they first arrived. The man always seemed to leave a trail of blood behind him.

And none of that blood ever came from his veins.

12

AS THEY DROVE DOWN off the mountain into the valley, the garishly-lit town of Las Vegas greeted them. The temperature in the desert that Friday night was eighty-five. The daytime had seen the thermometer soar to one hundred and twelve.

The lights of the town glittered in the clear desert sky. Kenyatta leaned forward and took in the sight. Memories of his desert plane crash flooded his mind. Visions of the ranch and the beautiful white woman who had made her intentions very clear drew a surge from his loins.

Elliot Stone battled the strong desert winds, keeping the car far from the right-hand side of the two-lane highway. His heart was pounding now as he drove down the hill and into the city.

"Man," Stone said, "that's some sight!"

"Uh huh," Kenyatta replied. "An' that fucker ain't never goin' be the same after we get through with it!"

The words sent a chill up Stone's spine. They were the invaders, approaching their objective. Single-handedly they would attempt to smash the power structure that supplied heroin to the men, women, and children of Watts, two hundred and eighty-five miles to the southwest. In the midst of the pretty neon lights and happy people was a vicious operation, a death-dealing force that had taken the lives of more men and women, mostly black, than Stone or Kenyatta would ever know about.

"You know," Stone said, "when I was a kid, I always wanted to make it to this town. I mean, I dug the whole scene—lights, music, beautiful chicks. It seemed like some kind of dream place to me, you dig?"

Kenyatta nodded. He looked at the handsome black man driving the car and realized for the first time in a long time just how young Stone was. "Yeah, I can dig it," Kenyatta replied.

Stone chuckled. "An' now, we're hittin' the fuck-er. Only it ain't for fun and games. We're comin' here to kill, Kenyatta. I mean, this is the first time I've ever made it to Vegas, man!"

Kenyatta laughed, turned, and glanced at Chamus curled up on the backseat, sound asleep. "Man," Kenyatta said, "we're comin' here to get rid of a killer, not to kill. Dudes like our fucker in the back and his men, they're the killers. We just tryin' to keep our people alive long enough so they can make it. Dead niggers don't do no one no good, you dig where I'm comin' from?"

The signs along the highway leading into the city announced the appearance of Frank Sinatra in an opening night at Caesar's Palace the next evening. Kenyatta looked at each one of these, and the idea grew in his mind steadily.

"Man," he said to Stone, "Sinatra's goin' be doin' a gig here tomorrow night."

Stone nodded and waited for Kenyatta to continue.

"You ever hear what comes down when Ol' Blue Eyes plays? Well, I'll tell you, Elliot. The whole fuckin' town goes bananas. The big spenders come in from all over, the high rollers. The organization's boys all jam that theater to hear him..., it's one of the real happenings. You dig where I'm comin' from?"

Stone shook his head. He wasn't sure what Kenyatta was leading up to.

"Okay, man," Kenyatta said. "The town empties, makes it over to where he's opening, right? I mean, the big boys from all over town. So while he's singing his songs, man, we strike!"

"Uh huh," Stone replied. "I can dig it, Kenyatta. But we make a hit right down the street, man, and those cats'll be right on top of us!"

"It depends, Elliot," Kenyatta replied "I mean, we don't know where the meeting's takin' place, right? No matter. As long as it's in the town and not on the

fuckin' desert somewheres, we'll be dealin' with a lot
less security. They'll be coverin' Sinatra and his audience."

"Man," Stone chuckled, "seems like everythin's
workin' right down the line for us. I mean, it seems
like a stroke of pretty fine luck headin' our way, you
dig?"

Kenyatta smiled. "Sometimes, Elliot, things just
come together in such a way as to make you believe
there's a little somethin' else on your side."

Stone turned and glanced at the tall, bald-headed
black man. There were always more sides to Kenyatta
than the black leader would let on to. And it always
surprised Stone when he would reveal another aspect
to him.

It took Kenyatta and Stone a couple of hours to find
a room in the jammed town. But finally they located
one in a small motel in the northern section, just past
downtown, which was called "The Palms." Rufus and
Edgar, following directly behind in the Chevy, took
the room next door, and the small group settled in.

Inside the room, Kenyatta tied Chamus to the corner of the bed, then sent Rufus out for a bottle of Jack
Daniels and some fried chicken. The air conditioner
droned on, and the men made themselves comfortable.

"All right, my man," Kenyatta began, sitting on the
overstuffed chair in the corner of the room, "it's about
time you made your little call. You dig where I'm
comin' from?"

Wilbur Chamus looked up at Kenyatta, staring balefully at the large black man who had come to mean certain death to the former L.A. hustler. "Man," Chamus began in his high-pitched voice, "you got yourself a thing goin'. Please, lemme out an' I'll make sure you're taken care of."

Kenyatta glanced toward Stone and laughed loudly. "Can you dig this dude, Elliot? The man is about ready to sink an' he's beggin' for his fuckin' life! I seen some dudes in my time, but this one is about the biggest motherfucker of all."

Elliot Stone moved across the room to where Chamus lay on the floor. He stood above the thin black man and stared down at him with a look that would have melted an iceberg. "Chamus," Stone began in an even colder voice, "you been makin' my man uptight. Now, I suggest you do as he says, lest you wanna die a death the likes of which you couldn't imagine!"

Kenyatta watched Chamus, then raised the glass of Jack Daniels to his lips and took a huge swig. He had seen men in the throes of terror before, and most men would react in much the same way. It was the common, unspoken admission of pure terror and horror. A man could only go on for so long before his control gave out. Chamus' had just evaporated.

"Now listen, man," Kenyatta began softly, "we ain't goin' hurt you. Just make that call. Set it up, you dig?"

Chamus looked pleadingly at Kenyatta. "Man, you don't know those people. You got the number, you call them. I got to get out, Kenyatta. They'll kill me!"

Kenyatta lifted himself off the chair and moved beside Stone. Both men stared down at the pathetic figure. "Elliot," Kenyatta began, "this dude is beggin' for his life. I just wonder how many poor fuckers he's responsible for killin' just so he could wear these fine threads that he's just pissed in like a schoolchild."

"Ain't no way to tell, Ken," Stone replied. "Man's pushed a lot of dope into our community. A whole lot."

Chamus looked from one to the other, realizing that there was no chance for him with men like these. All his life, the ghetto pusher had been dealing with men who could be bought, men to whom the dollar was the common denominator of all existence. Once a man left that realm, dudes like Chamus were incapable of understanding them, let alone dealing with them.

"Well," Kenyatta said finally, "looks like our man has a choice. I mean, we either cut his balls off right here or we give him the chance to make that call. Pretty good fuckin' choice, if you ask me."

The thin black man cringed. "Okay, man, I'll make the fuckin' call."

Kenyatta turned and went back to his chair. Stone reached for the phone, tapped for an outside number, and gave the receiver to Chamus. As Chamus asked the operator to dial the number, Kenyatta listened, making sure it was the same one that Manning had given him out on the desert earlier that night.

Chamus spoke with his man for a minute, then held the receiver away from his ear. "He wants to meet at the sand dunes, ten miles north of here."

Kenyatta shook his head. "No way. We meet at his place, where he lives, or we don't meet at all."

Chamus relayed the message. Finally, he nodded his head and turned back to Kenyatta. "Ten, tomorrow night," he said.

"Uh uh. Shit, we make it at midnight," Kenyatta replied.

After a few more minutes on the phone, Chamus reached an agreement. He hung up the phone and turned to Kenyatta. "Midnight, tomorrow night. The Sands Hotel. The penthouse suite."

Stone whistled. "Penthouse suite, eh? That's too much, man. From the fuckin' streets of Watts to a penthouse suite in Vegas. Man, I'd never thought I'd make it!"

Kenyatta laughed. "Elliot, baby, you have made it. Only fuckers around here who aren't goin' to make it are the goddamn pusher men!"

Chamus sat on the floor. His hand rested on the telephone. His black knuckles were white. He was gripping the plastic machine as though it was the last thing on earth he would ever touch. He tried to think, attempted to come up with some way of getting himself out of what was coming down. But no matter how hard he tried, there was nothing. His mind had been paralyzed with fear.

While Chamus sat alone, drifting into a state of complete fear, Rufus and Edgar returned with the fried chicken. The four men turned on the television set, watched a baseball game, and ate and drank as though they were in Las Vegas with the same intention of having fun that everyone else in town had.

While Kenyatta and his men sat in their room at

the Palms Motel, a virtual caravan of automobiles was heading up the four-lane freeway out of Los Angeles and into Las Vegas. Kenyatta's men in the districts of L.A. had gathered after the leader's message had been received from Barstow earlier that evening. Preparations had already been made by Stonewall, and the various groups of men within the organization had been gathering since early that Friday.

All told, the group consisted of thirty-eight black men, all of them indoctrinated into Kenyatta's philosophy, most of them with families, and all of them highly trained in the use of weapons.

Outside Stonewall's home, the eight automobiles were parked. In the trunks of each was a small arsenal—pistols, rifles, and shotguns. The men moved quietly and efficiently in the quiet neighborhood street in Compton. They did not want to draw attention to themselves. Black men with more than two cars at one time always drew attention, no matter how innocent their activity. On this night, their activities were something a little more than innocent, and they tried to be careful.

By eleven o'clock, the caravan was ready. Each car left, carrying at least four men dressed in business suits, toward Las Vegas. Half the cars took the desert route through Lancaster and Mojave. The other half rode the San Bernardino Freeway, then cut over the Angeles Mountains and down into the desert town of Victorville.

At about four in the morning, the eight cars would enter the town of Las Vegas. Each of the passengers would be dropped at a different casino, where they would have a little breakfast and play the slot machines. The men would wait there until the drivers came back and picked them up. When that pickup would occur would depend upon Kenyatta, who would meet with his four district leaders in a small coffee shop on the outskirts of the desert town.

After making sure the cars and men were inconspicuously slotted in the many casinos throughout town, Stonewall drove up Las Vegas Boulevard, past the luxurious Strip hotels, and headed through the downtown area. Finally he reached the Palms Motel and pulled into the parking lot next to Kenyatta's Cadillac.

Kenyatta was inside the room watching a late-night western on television and sipping his Jack Daniels. Elliot Stone was asleep on the couch, and Chamus was curled up on the floor, his hands and feet bound to the bed. Kenyatta flinched at the first knock on the door, then bounded to his feet, pulling out his .38 and holding it at his side. "Yeah?" he asked.

Stonewall identified himself, and Kenyatta opened the door. The two sat opposite each other in front of the television, speaking in whispers.

"Everyone here?" Kenyatta asked.

"Yeah, we took separate routes. They're spread out all around town just waitin' for the word."

Kenyatta paused as he filled Stonewall's glass with some whiskey. The tall, slim black man raised his glass and saluted Kenyatta.

"Ken," Stonewall began after taking a long swig,

"you got to level with me."

"Sure, man, I dig where you're comin' from," Kenyatta replied.

"Who is it, man? I mean, we got ourselves a fuckin' army in this town, and ain't no one knows what it's about. You dig?"

Kenyatta set his glass down on the small table. "Stonewall, we don't know who the shit this fucker is. All we know is that we're meetin' at the Sands tomorrow night. Midnight. The same time Sinatra opens at Caesar's. Aside from that, and possibly our little pusher friend down there, no one knows nothin'."

Stonewall leaned back in his chair. "You mean, you got this contact goin' at the Sands? The dude must be big, man."

"Got to be," Kenyatta replied. "Ain't no way a man corners a market like L.A. an' ain't big. You dig?"

"Yeah," Stonewall mused, staring down at his hands. "I just wonder…. I mean, the dude's that big. We walkin' into some fuckin' trap or what?"

Kenyatta shrugged, then leaned forward, earnestly looking Stonewall in the eyes. "Man, we come this far, this close. We got close to forty men out there ready and willin'. We ain't never been in a better position to get it on than we are now."

"You're right, Ken," Stonewall replied. "But we got to be careful."

The large, bald black man reached for a cigarette and lit it. He exhaled the smoke slowly and thoughtfully. "Who we got at the Sands? I mean, right now?"

Stonewall thought a moment, then said, "Roscoe Baker, good young dude out of Compton."

"Can you get in touch with him?" Kenyatta asked. "I mean, right now?"

"Sure. We got a code. I page him, then tell him Gloria is ready. He comes out to the parking lot fifteen minutes later."

Kenyatta smiled. "Okay, page him now."

While Stonewall paged Baker at the Sands, Kenyatta woke up Stone. He told him to watch the place for an hour. Quickly, Elliot Stone jumped into a state of total alertness, another aspect of his training with Kenyatta.

Kenyatta and Stonewall climbed into the Cadillac and headed toward the Strip. When they reached the Sands, they pulled into the parking lot near the large fountain.

"How long's it been?" Kenyatta asked when they had waited for a few minutes.

Stonewall checked his watch. "Should be any second," he replied.

At that moment, a young, hip-looking black dude with a stylish Afro appeared at the doorway, scanning the parking lot. He spotted the large Cadillac and ambled across the pavement toward Kenyatta and Stonewall. Roscoe Baker peered into the car, recognized Stonewall, and climbed into the backseat.

"What's happenin'?" Baker asked in a low, easy voice.

"This here," Stonewall began, "is Kenyatta."

The reaction was potent as Baker reached across

the seat and grasped Kenyatta's hand in a thumb
shake. "Man," Baker said, "it's a groove!"

"Same here," Kenyatta replied.

"We need some work done, and quick." Stonewall
began.

"Right," Kenyatta continued. "We need you to go
inside the Sands, check out everything you can about
the place—the elevators, the access to the penthouse,
where the security guards are, the back entrances, ser-
vants' entrances, everything. You dig where I'm
comin' from?"

Baker nodded, then looked toward Stonewall.
"Then what?" the young black asked.

"Then," Stonewall replied, "you grab a taxi and
have him take you to the Palms Motel on North Las
Vegas Drive. Room sixteen. We'll be there waitin'."

Baker nodded, then turned to Kenyatta. "I'll be
there in an hour, Kenyatta."

"Good man," Kenyatta smiled, then shook the
young man's hand. In a flash, Baker was out of the
car and gliding across the lot as though he were a
young stud on the prowl. Kenyatta watched him for
a moment, then turned to Stonewall. "Looks like a
righteous dude," he said.

"All our cats," Stonewall said, "are righteous
dudes."

Kenyatta looked at his old friend and smiled. He
drove through the parking lot and headed back to the
small motel.

Within an hour, Roscoe Baker appeared at the
motel. Elliot Stone opened the door and escorted him

inside. They turned on the lights and gathered around the small desk table in the center of the room. Chamus watched the men from the floor, powerless to do or say anything.

Baker squatted among the group of men, spreading out a large piece of notebook paper upon which he had drawn a map and diagram of the Sands Hotel. "This," Baker began, "is the Sands first floor. It's as far as the honkies would let me get. But I got enough."

Kenyatta stared at the map, tracing the rear hallways that ran behind the casino, and the entrances that were behind the hotel. The front elevators and lobby were impossible. What he was after was a more accessible route. Some way to get to the top.

"See," Baker continued, pointing out the rear parking lot. "The loading docks for food are here. Elevators to the third-floor kitchen are right there."

Stone smiled at Kenyatta, then spoke. "Ken, if those fuckin' elevators go to the kitchen on the third floor, they must have chutes goin' all the way to the top. I mean, room service and all that shit. You dig where I'm comin' from?"

"No doubt," Kenyatta said excitedly. "Got to be chutes. I think we got our way inside."

Chamus watched the men closely, listened to their conversation, and began to tremble again. His one hope, his one outside chance at survival, would be if Kenyatta could not get his men into the hotel. If that was prevented, then it would be possible for Chamus to sound some kind of warning when he met with Oscar Manning. Otherwise, chaos would ensue and surely Chamus would become a victim.

Outside the small motel room, the sun was rising over the desert. Rays of pink sunshine poured into the room illuminating the faces of the men gathered there with a strange, orange glow. The half-empty bottle of Jack Daniels sat on the desk beside the map of the Sands. Kenyatta, Stone, Baker, and Stonewall sat facing one another, sipping slowly on their drinks.

The excitement and the tension were building, and the men gathered inside the room were feeling it. Each man was sitting back as the sun rose, in his own mind contemplating what was to happen some eighteen hours from that moment.

Each man knew that this was the biggest attempt at anything he had ever been involved in. The soothing desert sunrise only made their feelings of anticipation and apprehension that much more real.

13

BY FOUR O'CLOCK that afternoon, every motel and hotel room in Las Vegas was filled. Thousands of normal, everyday people had converged on the desert town, along with hundreds of wealthy, crap-shooting white men. Frank Sinatra was opening that evening in a gala twelve o'clock show. And when Sinatra opened in Vegas, the high rollers gathered, along with the not-so-high rollers who enjoyed rubbing elbows with the rich.

The Strip itself was jammed with people as the sun began making its descent in the western sky. The air was dry and hot, and a soft wind blew from the north. In front of Caesar's Palace, where huge fountains

spurted forth tons of water, thousands of people had
gathered. They stood around, dressed in casual poly-
esters and double knits, waiting for a glimpse of the
king, or maybe the opportunity of spotting some
famous celebrity.

As the evening progressed toward midnight, the
other casinos and rooms around the Strip would grad-
ually empty, the throngs gathering in front of the
Palace. They all wanted to be where the action was.

Kenyatta continued to stare at the happy, thronging
people as they drove past. "Man," he began softly,
"someday I'd like to come up here, catch a show,
bring Betty..., shoot a little craps. You know?"

Elliot Stone did know. They had both resolved
themselves to spending the rest of their lives looking
in from the outside. Neither man would ever know
what the good life was about, what it would be like
to live a normal, violence-free life.

"Sometimes," Stone said after a long silence, "all
this shit, the lights, the beautiful broads, all of it makes
you forget where things are really at."

Kenyatta nodded. Then he quickly lit a cigarette
and his face became frozen into a mask of determination and purpose.

Stone drove down to the Hacienda at the far end of
the Strip, turned around, and headed back toward the
downtown area and the motel. They would take in a
good dinner, but no drinking and no heavy foods, just
a steak and a salad. After that, they would shower and
shave. Then, like the toreadors of Spain, they would
dress themselves carefully and purposefully. Every

move, every normal activity from that moment on would be concentrated upon and done with incredible directness. No man really knew whether or not this would be his last day on earth.

At eleven o'clock that night, Stonewall began making the rounds of the various hotels and casinos on the Strip. Each group of men was gathered together and put into one of the eight cars that had come up to Las Vegas. Within twenty minutes, Kenyatta's massive gang was assembled and ready to go.

At the Palms Motel, Kenyatta untied Wilbur Chamus and allowed the former pusher to change his clothes. The slim black man trembled as he donned a tight-fitting turtleneck and mohair slacks. Kenyatta and Stone, along with Rufus and Edgar, waited for the man until he finished. Finally, Chamus looked a little more like his old self—dapper, mean, and ready to deal.

"Everyone check their arms?" Kenyatta asked.

"We got it all, Kenyatta," Stone replied, flashing the huge .45 he carried.

"Okay, gentlemen," Kenyatta said, leading the way out the door. "We got ourselves some work to do!"

Kenyatta, Stone, and Chamus climbed into the Cadillac. In the trunk was an empty suitcase, supposedly filled with the heroin. But the white powder was still sealed tightly in the lining of the roof. Kenyatta was taking no chances. Even if he lost, he would make sure the smack would never reach the wrong hands.

Elliot Stone turned out on Las Vegas Boulevard and

headed toward downtown. As they passed through the garishly-lit center, Rufus and Edgar joined them in the rear, driving the Chevrolet.

The Strip was virtually empty. It was fifteen minutes to twelve, and far up the street in front of Caesar's Palace, Kenyatta and Stone could see the milling throng.

"Man," Kenyatta exclaimed, "we sure picked a righteous hour!"

Stone laughed nervously. The tension was building to a peak inside him. "Just keep those people away from here and we'll be all right."

The Sands was quiet, as were the rest of the hotels on the Strip. Stone pulled into the lot in front and parked the car in the self-serve area. Quickly he and Kenyatta jumped out, then waited for Chamus.

"One wrong blink of your eye, Chamus," Kenyatta threatened coldly, "an' I'm gonna blow your fuckin' head off!"

There was no need to threaten the black man. His nerves had been shattered for some time. Nothing was going to make him take a chance now.

Slowly the three men walked toward the entrance of the hotel. Kenyatta carried the suitcase and kept his other hand ready to go inside his coat for his .38.

At that moment, in the rear of the hotel, four cars slowly cruised the parking lot. One stopped in a space near the service entrance, while another pulled into the small slot next to the loading dock. The other two pulled into customers' slots.

Four men climbed out of each car. Some of them

walked stiffly, as though limping. Sawed-off shotguns were held firmly beneath their jackets.

At the other end of the building, near the pool area, another four cars stopped and dropped off their passengers. These men scampered across the small putting green and toward the patio. They leaped the small fence outside and made their way toward the service elevators.

As each man had been picked up along the route, Stonewall had explained quickly the general layout of the hotel. The only routes up to the penthouse would be through the service elevators and the kitchen elevator. According to the diagram drawn up by Roscoe Baker, the men would have to enter the building through the side and the rear, somehow make their way to the elevator, and get to the top. The rest would be up to them.

Kenyatta, Stone, and Chamus walked quickly through the lobby toward the main elevator. Inside, Kenyatta pushed the button for the penthouse. Before the doors closed, a voice came over the intercom inside the cubicle asking who was calling.

"Chamus...," Kenyatta replied. Then added, "and friends."

"Okay," the voice replied, "come on up."

The doors closed and the elevator began its ascent to the penthouse suite.

Clement Jenkins stood with his back to the door, staring out at the skyline of Las Vegas. Oscar Manning sat on the couch, nervously puffing on a cigarette. Two other men, both white, stood at attention at either side of the large, plush penthouse.

The elevator arrived at the top floor and Kenyatta and Stone were greeted by a tall, broad-shouldered white man in a neat business suit. He looked at both men, then down at Chamus.

"He'll see you now," the white man said.

Kenyatta nodded, then gave Chamus a slight nudge and pushed him out into the red velvet hallway. Stone followed immediately behind as the white man led the way to the gold-plated door at the end of the hall. As he approached the door, Kenyatta turned quickly and glanced down toward the other end. There the service elevator doors remained shut. He prayed silently that his men were inside and on their way. He would not have much time with the man inside the penthouse.

The white man opened the doors to Jenkins' suite and ushered Kenyatta and Stone inside. Chamus followed a few steps behind the two men.

Clement Jenkins turned from the window and stared at Stone and Kenyatta with cold, blue eyes. His mouth was set in a frown, and the maroon dinner jacket he wore did not add much to change the sour aura. "Welcome to Las Vegas, gentlemen," he said coldly.

"Pleasure's mine, sir," Kenyatta replied quickly. His first look at this man who caused so much death and heartbreak did not jive with his hatred. The man, thought Kenyatta, was nothing more than a weak white man. A white who had had the benefit of the best education, the most money, and all the opportunities.

All he had done was live his life as it had been set

for him to walk through it. Kenyatta continued to stare at the slim, feeble-looking Jenkins, then suddenly understood why he disliked the man. Jenkins smelled of death. There was nothing about him that suggested he had ever lived, or that he ever had any intentions of living. The man, thought Kenyatta, was a death dealer.

"Let's get on with it," Jenkins said after Stone and Kenyatta sat down on the plush couch. "You know I've missed Frank's opening because of this."

Kenyatta nodded. "Yeah, well, we're really sorry 'bout that."

Stone sat on the edge of the couch waiting. He knew that Kenyatta would have to make the first move and that everyone was waiting for the first sound of gunfire. After that, he knew that all hell would break loose.

Kenyatta leaned back on the couch and lit a cigarette. He looked directly at Clement Jenkins and smiled. "Your man out there on the desert, mister, offered seven-five. Well, the price goin' to go up a little bit. All this travelin' an' shit."

Jenkins strode across the room and took a seat behind his huge oak desk. Obviously, the mammoth thing gave him a sense of power. "All right, what's the price?"

"One flat, mister. One million dollars in cold, hard cash."

There was a silence in the room. Jenkins looked first to Manning, then to Chamus. Both men looked away. Finally, he turned back to Kenyatta. "You fuckin' little jungle bunny! You come waltzing in here and demand a price like that! I'm surprised your weak little mind can even conceive of such a high number!"

Kenyatta felt his blood boiling. "You mean you won't take it for that price?" he said, trying to sound cool.

"You asshole nigger! What kind of fool do you think I am, boy?"

For the first time in his life, Kenyatta knew that he had underestimated his man.

14

STONEWALL STOOD WITH HIS back against the wall of the elevator. There were sixteen black men jammed into the small cubicle riding slowly toward the penthouse suite. They had managed to sneak by the two security guards outside the kitchen, then to make it through the cooking area itself. Once at the elevators, they were safe. Now, with guns drawn and ready, they were riding to the top of the Sands Hotel, where they would fight the battle of their lives.

At the top of the elevator chute, suspended by harnesses from the gear system, were two white men, both employees of Clement Jenkins, and each of them held a tear-gas rifle pointed down the shaft at the roof of the approaching elevator. The two men waited, held their rifles at the ready, and finally heard what they had been waiting for. Two short knocks on the elevator door from outside where the penthouse hallway was.

Each man fired his rifle. The explosion was muted by the tiny area of the chute and by the noise of the gears above them.

The two pellets from the rifles entered the elevator, quickly making two tiny holes in the roof as they passed through the wood. When the pellets hit the floor, they exploded again, creating a small, invisible cloud of nerve gas CL-809.

One of Clement Jenkins' more lucrative businesses was the development of nerve gases for the United States Army. But his mission was anything but patriotic. As soon as he developed a newer, more lethal gas for the U.S., he would turn around and sell that same gas to Russia. CL-809 was the most lethal yet, creating an instant spasm of the nervous system, causing instant suffocation through strangulation. The beautiful part of CL-809 was that its effects lasted for only fifteen seconds. Then it was absorbed into the atmosphere and became harmless.

Neither Stonewall nor any of his men inside the elevator ever knew what hit him. In an orgy of convulsions, each man struggled for a split second to retain his life. But that had been only a motor reaction and not one from the brain. They were all dead before any one of them ever had the opportunity to realize that death was coming.

The two men who had done the shooting secured the elevator in its position by locking the gears, then crawled out of their little harnesses and opened the doors to the penthouse suite. The white man who had greeted Kenyatta and Stone stood in the hallway smiling.

Kenyatta's other group of men were hit at poolside near the side entrance to the hotel. After jumping the fences, they had made their way into the lounge area near the pool. There they were greeted by twenty heavily-armed white men. Each of the men carried a submachine gun, pointed directly at one of the black men.

The black men had not had a chance to shoot. They dropped their pistols and sawed-off shotguns onto the floor and allowed the white army to lead them into the sauna room. Nineteen of Kenyatta's best men were herded into the small cubicle used to sweat off the fat and blubber of wealthy white men. None of the black men needed to lose a pound from their young, strong frames.

The leader of the whites shoved the last black man into the sauna room. Before closing the door, he tossed in a small capsule, which exploded like a tiny firecracker upon hitting the ground.

The black men inside the room watched the little thing explode. It was the last thing any of them would ever see. Once again, Clement Jenkins had created a marvel.

No one in the room really saw either of the two

black men pull out the pistols. The first that anyone knew about it was through the retort of the gunshots as both men began firing.

Kenyatta took aim at Clement and fired. But the bullet struck the wood frame of the desk, bounced off, and struck Clement in the shoulder.

Elliot Stone knew he must knock off the two guards. He lifted his .45 and fired at the one next to the door attempting to get out his pistol. The bullet struck the man in the forehead. He flew backward, crashing against the wood and screaming out. Stone whirled off the couch and hit the floor, spinning his body around so that he could get a shot at the guard who was standing next to him.

But the man was taking direct aim at the big black man. Kenyatta was holding his pistol out with two hands, pointing the gun at Clement's desk. But the white man had fallen to the floor when he was struck by the first bullet. Kenyatta was waiting for the man to crawl out from behind his desk. He wanted to see the white man crawl, the white millionaire who dealt in death. He wanted to see him crawling on his hands and knees, begging for some kind of mercy. Kenyatta would wait all night to see it, to see a man whom he had hated in the abstract for so many years beg him for his life.

But Kenyatta was not to see this. The guard in the corner of the room pulled the trigger of his .45. The bullet struck Kenyatta in the back of the head, sending pieces of his shattered skull flying against Clement's oak desk. With half of his head shot away,

Kenyatta tumbled forward and fell onto the superb shag rug.

Elliot Stone knew where the bullet had gone. He had been aiming at the guard's stomach but now raised his sights to the man's eyes. He leveled his barrel, then pulled the trigger.

The guard froze for a moment as the right side of his face exploded into a mass of blood and eye tissue. His entire right side was oozing with brain matter. He stood there for a moment, his other eye wandering wildly in his skull, then fell back against the wall.

There was no time to think anymore for Elliot Stone. Manning and Chamus were huddled in the corner of the room. Both men, black and white, clutching at each other as though there was safety in their position. Stone raised his gun, looked into the terrified faces of both men, and fired twice.

Each man was struck in the neck. The cords and bone tissue erupted from their bodies as their heads were snapped backward with a sickening sound. As their heads rolled ungainly on their shoulders, they still clutched at each other, now locked tightly by the fear of death.

Suddenly, the penthouse was silent. Outside in the hallway, the two men from the elevator and the white man who had greeted them were trying to push the doors open. But the body of the guard was blocking their way.

Elliot Stone knew he had a few seconds left with the white man who lay wounded somewhere behind

the huge desk. Outside he could hear the roar of
engines, the sound of a huge machine being warmed
up. At first, Stone did not know what it was, but after
listening for a second, he recognized it as a helicopter.

Stone crept along the floor, around the couch, and
toward the huge desk. He knew that the white man
was armed now and that he would be killed if he faced
him point blank. He moved slowly, cautiously, then
threw down a corner table and used that as a shield.

"Come outta there, you bastard!" Stone demanded,
now lying next to the mutilated body of Kenyatta.

There was only silence from behind the desk.

"I'm tellin' you, man, come outta there!"

Nothing.

Suddenly, the doors burst open behind him. Stone
instinctively whirled onto his back and began firing.
He hit the white man squarely in the jaw with his first
bullet, sending him screaming into the hallway as he
was thrown backward.

The two men from the elevator shaft began firing
wantonly into the smoke-filled room. Stone fired off
two shots, one hitting one of them in the gut and the
other snapping his partner backward with a hit to his
shoulder.

In the madness of the gunfire, Elliot Stone was hit
in the leg. He felt the bullet enter a spot just below
his bad knee. For a moment, his mind clouded and he
was traveling back in time to the football field, the
day he had been injured. The pain was just as great
then, just as powerful. But now, lying back against
the body of Kenyatta, he felt as though he would not

survive this one. That other time a crowd had cheered him. His teammates had gathered around him to give him words of encouragement.

It was different this time. His only friend, the only black man he had come to really know and respect, was lying dead next to him on the floor.

A warm gust of air and the thunderous sound of a helicopter engine drew Stone out of his delirium. He sat up on the floor, still clutching his leg. He turned and looked out the picture window. The windows in the suite were open and the warm desert air was blowing into the death-filled room.

Crawling, half-walking, Stone made his way to the window. Outside was a small patio. But off to the right was a huge space, the roof of the hotel.

On the roof was a helicopter. Clement Jenkins was staggering toward the machine, trying with all his energy to make it to safety.

"You bastard!" Stone cried as he ran out onto the patio and toward the waiting chopper. The young black held his gun pointed toward Jenkins—waiting, just waiting to get within range.

Finally, Stone was within shooting distance. Jenkins was at the side of the helicopter, struggling to get up into the open doorway.

Stone fired. A man fell from inside the helicopter and rolled behind Jenkins onto the ground. Suddenly, two sets of arms lifted Jenkins into the darkness of the helicopter.

Elliot Stone moved as quickly as he could across the roof. The black before him, like the blackness of the Notre Dame line, loomed as a challenge. The former running back moved through the jungle toward the open field.

But the darkness remained. The helicopter was now fifteen, then twenty, then thirty feet above his head. Stone fired at the machine, using his last bullet. But the bullet shot into the night sky, traveling to infinity.

The last glimpse Elliot Stone had of the chopper was one he would never forget. The half-smiling, half-frightened face of the small, thin white man. It was a ghostly image that peered from within the darkness of the chopper down at Stone—the image of a man who had won again, yet who knew his time was coming.

Suddenly, the night became real again—the strong wind blowing off the desert, the lights of Las Vegas below, and the penthouse suite across the rooftop. Stone turned, not knowing where to go, and saw the room filled with armed men running around excitedly.

Kenyatta was still there, and Stone wanted to go back, but he knew no matter what he did in his lifetime he could never bring the big man back. He knew he must run.

Using the fire escape on the side of the hotel, Elliot Stone managed to escape the small army of Clement Jenkins. The parking lot in front of the Sands was quiet. Stone had expected police to be swarming the place. Instead, just a few late-night strollers passed nearby.

Trying to cover his wound, Stone limped to where

they had left the Cadillac. He fished inside his pockets for the keys and climbed inside the car. A half-filled bottle of Jack Daniels lay in the glove compartment, and the young black took a long, strong swig. He started the car and drove out onto Las Vegas Boulevard.

As he drove out along the Strip, he passed Caesar's Palace. Huge crowds milled around the fountains in front, talking and laughing in the warm desert night.

Elliot Stone clutched his leg and tried to stop the bleeding. It would be a long, nightmarish drive through the desert back to Los Angeles.

Detectives Benson and Ryan peeled off their suit jackets and threw them into the front seat of their car. The desert heat was incredible, reaching over one hundred and twenty. It was always hotter in the flatlands a hundred miles north of Las Vegas.

The two detectives greeted the highway patrolman and the two special agents of the FBI as they walked across a small sand dune toward a ravine. The five men stood on the crest of the ravine and stared down.

Two bodies, both black men, lay side by side in the sand. Next to them stood two officers of the Nevada State Police.

"Blacks are always being found out here," the state trooper said to Benson.

"Not like this one," Benson replied curtly.

The trooper watched as Benson and Ryan ran down the steep side of the ravine and approached the bodies.

Both men stood above the dead body of Kenyatta. Flies were eating away at the black man's shattered skull. His brain matter had turned a sickly green and was still oozing from the wound.

"My God!" Benson said softly.

Ryan looked at his partner. He knew what he was thinking, because he had been thinking the same thing. Deep inside, both men knew that the wrong man was lying on the desert.

But neither man knew who the right man was.

Donald Goines
SPECIAL PREVIEW

SWAMP MAN

This preview will introduce you to George Jackson, a "Swamp Man," born and bred in the dark watery woods of Mississippi. He was a gentle young man who turned as deadly as a water moccasin after he saw what the four hill boys did to his sister. They caught her soon after she got off the bus, home from her first year of college. When they were through with her, she let her mind shut down, fearing to remember. Slipping through the swamps like a ghost, George stalked them, one by one, two by two....

I

THE SUN HAD JUST COME up when George Jackson pushed back some of the tall brown willow weeds he was hiding behind. He could now make out some of the wild ducks swimming in the creek. Even with the appearance of the sun over the tree tops it was still dark in the Mississippi swamp. George decided to wait until it became lighter before trying for one of the geese.

A tall, husky boy of fourteen, George already had the build of a man. It was evident that he would be an exceptionally powerful man when he was full grown. Suddenly he grew tense. An alarm inside of him started to tick. It was his swamp sense and told him that danger was near. His huge shoulders became tense; a large vein in his neck began to swell. His eyes darted back and forth. Not a muscle moved. He could have passed for a wooden statue.

As George's huge hands inched toward the trigger on the shotgun, he saw the danger approaching out of the corner of his eye. The deadly water moccasin was already three feet out of the water and halfway up the narrow bank.

The large poisonous snake had become intrigued with the warm-blooded creature it smelled. And as George watched, the snake started to slither toward him. He couldn't help but admire the way the reptile seemed to glide over the broken surface of the slimy ground.

George would have been in trouble if he hadn't been a swamp man. Before his father's death, the man had taken his son deep into the swamps, revealing byways to the young boy that were known by only a handful of men.

Suddenly the snake changed its course and went around him. George watched it enter the water, then go under. He smiled to himself as he realized what was happening. The snake was lying in ambush. If George should step anywhere near where the snake had hidden, he would be taking a chance on getting bitten. His eyes drifted over to the small dugout, checking to make sure none of the moccasin's brothers had taken an interest in his homemade canoe. But there was only the thin paddle and a stick eight feet long, important to the survival of any man who frequented the dangerous back waters.

It was now light enough to shoot. George raised the shotgun to his shoulder. He could see four ducks swimming together. Then he pulled the trigger. The gunshot rang out in the stillness of the morning. He rushed over to his dugout, his boots making a swishy sound as he ran through the slime. He moved now by instinct, pushing out into the water, keeping his eyes on the two birds that he knew he had killed.

Before the sound of the gunshot had died, the other birds had taken to the wing. One could hear the rustle from the trees as other animals and birds took flight. The gunshot warned them that their most dangerous enemy was near.

George had one problem now confronting him. If he didn't reach his birds in time, one of the other carnivorous beasts of prey might beat him to his meal. He didn't have to worry about the alligators. They had been hunted too much by man. They were cautious now, lying on their mounds of earth and sunning themselves. Then, at the first warning of the approach of man, they would slide into the murky water and disappear. George thought about the alligators as he reached out and pulled in his first bird. With his long pole, he pulled the other one closer, then reached out and scooped it out of the water.

George remembered how it used to be when his father had first started bringing him into the swamps. 'Gators used to be everywhere. Now, you had to hunt them down. It wasn't a hard task for a person like George, but 'gator hunting was a job he didn't like.

He could stand snakes, but alligators he disliked. It was the way they dragged their victims underneath the water and buried them, waiting until the corpse became rotten. That was the way they liked their meat—stinking to high heaven. The thought of such a death filled him with dread.

George shook his head, trying to shake off the bad thoughts. This should be a day of happiness. His older sister would be coming home from college today. She had written last week and said she would come home for a visit. It would be the first time in two years, ever since she had received her scholarship from Lincoln College. It had taken some doing, or so she had said, but she had finally gotten one. It was a way to get out of the swamps—away from the white trash she had always despised. Even before the murder of their father, she had hated the southern whites, never speaking to them when they passed on the road.

George used his eight-foot pole to push the small dugout along faster. He passed the first cotton patch, which meant that he was getting out of the swamp. The cotton stalks were bent and broken. The small patch obviously wasn't being cared for. George knew why that was. This was an old cotton patch, and it had been worked by blacks. The little field was too deep into the swamps for the whites to really care about it. His grandfather used to tend the place, but he was too old now, and George, next to hating alligators, hated cotton, so the field went untended. The white trash, using the cotton as their bridge to the past, acted like old slave masters and got away with it.

There was a small cornfield up ahead and George poled his boat toward it. He dragged it up to dry land and left it under a thicket of sycamore trees. It was quiet and clean under the tall trees, with just a small breeze shaking the limbs at the top.

George went into the field and picked the ripest ears of corn he could find, taking enough to last a few days. He carried them back and placed them in the dugout, again checking for snakes before putting his burden down. It was more from habit than anything else, but it was a good habit. Too many swamp people had died needlessly from being bitten by cottonmouths because they hadn't used their eyes. It was a habit his father had drilled into him—to always look—because in the swamps death could be waiting around the next bend.

As George pushed his small boat back into the water, the only sounds he could hear were those of the swamp. Frogs, crickets, an old owl in a tree somewhere. The noise was like a soothing massage. George gave one vigorous push with the long pole and the boat cut swiftly through the water.

The closer he got to home, the less caution he used. Just the thought of seeing his sister Henrietta again made his chest swell. He tried to remember how she looked the last time he had seen her. They were standing at the bus stop, waiting for the Greyhound bus. He had walked the five miles to town, carrying her two little suitcases. She could have managed without his aid, but he had wanted to go with her. There was a bond between them—a tie so deep that, while she

was away at college, she wrote twice a month, two
letters at the same time, so that he wouldn't have to
make a trip into town for nothing. She knew the way
the mail was held at the small post office, so she wrote
him according to that schedule. Every other Friday he
would go into town, and sure enough there would be
a letter for him. Sometimes she even mailed a few
dollars so he could buy the stamps to answer her letters. Sometimes she sent small lessons for him to do,
even though she knew he went to the small school on
Master Wilson's plantation. She was always trying to
teach him things herself.

"Boy," he said to himself, "you goin' bust your big
mouth wide open if you keep on grinnin'." He had
spoken the words out loud and before he had finished
talking, he knew he had made a mistake. Somebody
was coming around the bend on his left. It could only
be the Jones boys, he realized quickly, and if there
were any hillbillies he hated to come in contact with,
it was the Jones boys—four brothers who lived on the
high land, land that was swampland, but dry enough
to raise certain crops.

It was identical to what George's family did—
raised crops to live on at the edge of the swamps.
Only a few people lived like this. To most farmers, it
was a poor way to earn a living. But George's father
and grandfather had always said it was better than
sharecropping—farming the land on one of the plantations and living as a tenant.

This way, they were independent. If they didn't
want to work, they didn't have to. Nor did they have

to answer to anyone for what they did on the land. With a few chickens and pigs, a man could exist, but rarely did he see any cash money.

George eyed the bend to the right, which would take him down the lane that led to his house. He didn't believe he could make it before the loudmouthed Jones boys came around from the opposite side.

And then they appeared. There were only two of them in their faded gray dugout, and if ever men looked a certain part, they looked theirs. White trash was written all over them. If this had been in the time of slavery, they would have been patrollers, men who ran down runaway slaves. Or, if not that, then members of the Confederate army. But slavery had been outlawed over a hundred years ago, and these days the Jones boys had to settle for just being avid members of the Ku Klux Klan.

Both men had long, stringy, dirty blond hair that hung down in their faces. They were always tossing their heads back so that they could get the hair out of their eyes. Both men had pale blue eyes, with eyebrows so light that from a distance it didn't seem as if they had any eyebrows at all. The only difference between the two brothers was age. The one sitting in the front of the boat was the youngest, still too green to grow a dirty, ill-shaped beard like his older brother.

"Nigger," the youngest Jones boy called out when they saw George, "ain't you got 'nough sense in that burr head not to be goin' 'round here talkin' to yourself?"

"Yes suh, Massah Jones," George answered, draw-

ing out the words in a practiced southern drawl. It
made the whitey's happy to be called master, but they
also wanted it said in the old southern drawl. If a
young black man wanted to get along with them, he
practiced this whenever he came in contact with them.
If not, he could bring trouble down on his head, or
on members of his family. And on occasions like this,
caught out in the swamps without any witnesses, only
a fool who didn't want to live to see tomorrow would
resort to the trick. The blacks joked amongst themselves about it, but the joke was on them. They joked
to take away the shame that they felt whenever they
had to resort to its use. But for George, it hurt worse
than ever. He had watched these same white men kill
his father, and now here he sat, grinning and calling
them "massah."

George thought about his sister. He had intended to
keep straight down the river so he could pick her up
if she came in today as she said she would. But now,
with the Jones boys going in that direction, he didn't
want to follow along too closely to them. He decided
to take the birds home first. Maybe Henrietta hadn't
caught the bus she had planned on catching, George
reasoned. But George knew deep down inside that his
reasoning was based on fear—the very real and urgent
fear he had of the men who had murdered his father.

"What you so happy for, boy?" the younger brother drawled. "'Cause Miss Nigger due this mornin'?"

"Jamie, shut your mouth, boy, if'n you don't want
my foot stuck down it!" the older brother stated harshly, cutting him off.

"That coon knows his place, Zeke," Jamie answered weakly, falling quickly into silence.

As George swung his boat into the bend on the right, his heart skipped a beat. They couldn't know, he thought. But then he realized that they did know. Old man Williams, who ran the post office, had been reading his mail again. There was no mistake, the Jones boys knew that Henrietta was due home today. Maybe that was the reason why they were on their way to town, just to abuse her verbally. That was all they could do, George believed. In a town full of people, what else could they possibly do to his sister. This was the sixties, not the turn of the century when honkies could get away with anything. Nowadays, they had to walk a pretty straight line. Of course, what they did in the back country without witnesses was something else. Black people made sure they didn't get caught alone in the back country. But for people like George, there was little choice. They lived in the wild back country, and their only source of protection was themselves.

George made the slanting right-hand turn into the S-shaped bend. The creek was much narrower here. There were trees on each side with long hanging vines. The green foliage on the left contrasted beautifully with the yellow of the tall cornfields swaying in the breeze. The morning smell of fresh air, mingled with the sweet chatter of birds, added still another dimension to the beauty of the river. But the young boy poling home did not notice these things. Under other circumstances, he might have stopped, stood up in the

boat, and inhaled deeply, enjoying the richness of
nature.

A heavy premonition was on him as he paddled out
of the last bend in the river's S-shaped curve and he
came within sight of his home. Actually, there were
two cabins. The first one stood high above the water
on heavy log stalks. The stilts were so massive it
seemed impossible that men had actually raised them.
But men had—and the home sitting on the river had
been the first cabin built on the land. George's father
and grandfather had then cleared the surrounding land
of stick brush, making the land ready for the planting
of crops. Each year they were able to harvest enough
corn, wheat, and vegetables to feed the family. With
the addition of wild meat and fish, the Jacksons were
able to survive off the land.

George tied the dugout near the ladder that led to
the catwalk. He had to push one of the other three
boats away. The heavy rowboat was used when they
had gone 'gator hunting, but George had discontinued
that when he became the only hunter in the family. It
was tied securely to the rear of the cabin by heavy
vines that were woven together to make a thick rope.
The other two boats were lighter dugouts similar in
construction to the one George was using. One was
built to carry at least three people, and the other one
was identical to the one George had just finished
securing to the dock.

George went up the ladder quickly, carrying only
his shotgun and the two dead birds. The crudely-made
catwalk swayed under his weight. He hurried toward

the ladder that led to dry ground. He had no reason to linger at the old house, because it was now used as a storage shack for fishing gear. Its other function was that of an outhouse, using the running water under the cabin to carry away the body waste. And what the water didn't get, the large, blackish-gray catfish that lingered underneath the cabin did.

The ground at the bottom of the ladder was firm. George ran up the well-used pathway, passing the few scattered trees on each side. The grass near the pathway was short, the weeds had been cleared out to prevent the snakes from hiding in the brush and striking out at those who used the pathway.

The distance to the new cabin on the high ground was a good two hundred yards. As George neared the cabin door, a tall, gaunt black man stepped out the door. The sunshine played tricks with the gray hair on the elderly man's head, trying to find a dark spot in the thinning gray curls. Eyeglasses sat on the edge of his nose, revealing eyes that were dark from sorrow, hurt, and regret. A lifetime of despair was written on the man's lean face. Three scars ran down the right side of his face, lashes from long ago, that now looked like wrinkles in the dark brown skin.

The old man stepped aside and let the young boy enter. Neither one spoke. From habit, the boy set the gun down at the door, then walked across the room and lay the birds on the crude handmade table.

As he turned to leave, George stopped and stared at the old man. "I'm goin' be needin' that, Pa."

George's grandfather continued on toward the table,

carrying the shotgun and a cleaning rag. "Old Jefferson," the old man began in a soft drawl, "he was workin' in them white folks' bar last night, when he hear them Jones trash talkin' 'bout our girl coming home." The old man, who only had a first name because his father refused to give his freeborn son a slave name, was known as Ben.

As he talked, Ben broke the gun down and reached for a rod. He glanced up at the boy who was quietly listening to him.

"You better be going, boy," Ben said, using the only term he ever used when speaking to George. It was a curious trait of the old man's. He would never use the boy's first or last name.

"I'm thinkin' I might need the shotgun, Pa," George stated quietly as he stood in front of the old man with his head down. He didn't want to look into those eyes because the boy was ashamed of his grandfather. Ashamed of the way his grandfather cringed when the whites were around. The old man couldn't help himself. He just shook. But the old man didn't tremble from fear. Instead, he shook from an inner rage, a feeling of frustration because he knew he was helpless.

"Not if'n yo' goin' after your sister. You goin' need both hands to help her with her bags," Ben stated as he rammed the rod down the barrel. Both man and boy knew what was not being said, that with whites you could never tell. The old man knew one thing for certain though and that was that the boy stood a better chance without the gun. He could tell that the boy had the same wild streak that his father had had. He was too quiet, staring out from his eyes at them as if to say there will be a judgment day.

"If'n you goin', boy, you better be hurryin'. She goin' be needin' your help," old Ben said, trying to make the boy go without the gun.

As George stared down at the old man, he fought back the rage to take the gun from him. It just wasn't in him to use violence against Pa. And he knew the old man would resist.

Without another word, George started toward the door. When he stepped outside, he started to run toward the dugout. The river would be the quickest way, landing at the big bend and walking the rest of the way. The youth pushed off and guided his dugout down the muddy waters of the Mississippi and toward his long-awaited reunion with his sister.

2

HENRIETTA WATCHED CLOSELY as the bus moved quickly through Buckwater, Mississippi. The population of the small town was two hundred, not counting the blacks. The few houses they passed were actually shacks. It would have been more appropriate to have called it Shanty Town. The crudely-made out-houses could be seen in the rear of each dwelling.

The sight of the town made Henrietta sick. How she despised the place. She thought of her talented brother with his ability to pick things up by himself. She remembered sending him the book on advanced math, thinking he could never understand it without some kind of help. Yet, reading slowly, he had learned from

the book. If there were only some way of taking him
out when I left, she thought. But their grandfather pre-
sented a problem. If she could talk the old man into
leaving, then it could work. Once back in Atlanta,
Georgia, she could get an agency to help. Then her
dream of getting little George out of that swamp
would come true.

The very thought of the swamp resurrected her
hatred for the place. Hate wasn't the word. Loathing
was more like it. The swamp was a loathsome thing,
like the creepy, crawly creatures that lived there.
Henrietta shivered and stood up as the bus parked in
front of the white-walled drugstore.

In front of the drugstore was a homemade, gray-
colored bench. Every day it was filled with the various
white men who had tramped in from the farms and
shanties. The drugstore also served as the hardware
store and was one of only two places you could buy
your supplies. Next to it was the log cabin post office
and the jail house. The street ended with the only bar
and the other general store. That section was always
busy at night when the two town whores were there.

Henrietta stepped from the bus with her two suitcases and looked around for George. She had just
known that he would be there. Something must have
happened, but what? She walked slowly past the staring men and stopped at the edge of the wooden walk.
The rest of the way was a dirt road leading toward
the trail out of town. If George was coming, that was
the way he would come.

As Henrietta watched for George, she noticed old

man Jefferson waving at her. She figured she could get the old man to help her with the two suitcases she had brought with her. She gathered up her luggage and ran across the street to where Jefferson stood. She didn't notice the frowns on the white men's faces, but Jefferson saw it and read a warning in it.

As she came hurrying over, the old man said quickly, "Gal, get back on the bus! Hurry, if'n yo' don't wanna have trouble out of them there crackers, 'cause they been sittin' and waitin' for yo' all mornin'."

"Why, that's impossible. They had no way of knowing. I'm sure you're just imagining things, Mr. Jefferson," she said lightly, not even considering getting back on the bus.

Jefferson shook his head. "Gal, I ain't foolin' with you. Go on now and get back on the bus."

She decided she had better take a firm hand with him. She had become used to working with elderly people from a job she held near the college at the Martin Luther King convalescent center for the elderly. Old people had a bad habit of getting bossy in their old age. Now here was this fool trying to order her back on the bus after she had endured that bumpy overnight ride.

Henrietta wasn't very tall, but she had a way of carrying herself and walking proud. She was slim, on the border of being skinny, yet she filled out the brown pants outfit she wore to perfection. Proud and haughty, that was the opinion of the men who watched her with interest.

"By God," Sonny-Boy Jones began, "that fuckin'

bitch is still stuck-up as hell! Gets off the bus like she owns this here town, sees us sittin' here, then got the uppity not to speak!"

"Aw now, Sonny. What you expect?" the short, muscular Earl Mason stated. Earl didn't bat an eye as Sonny turned on him. He stared into Sonny's cold, fishlike pale blue eyes and continued. "The gal witnessed the death of her pa before she left, so why the hell should she speak to some of the people she thinks killed him?" The breeze blew Earl's hair down in his face. He took his hand and pushed the reddish mass back out of his brown eyes.

Old man Turner, the owner of the general store, came out the door carrying a jug. "Yeah," he began, drawing the word out, making sure he held everybody's attention before he began to speak. "That old black gal done filled out a little since leavin'. Looks like she been eatin' wherever she been."

As the group of men watched and waited, old man Turner took his time about uncorking the jug. Every eye on the porch followed his motion as he tilted the jug up, swinging it over his forearm for support, and let the furious, burning corn liquor run down his throat like water. When he brought the jug back down, he patted his huge belly.

"A'llll," Turner groaned, "that's how you can tell good likker. It hits you in the gut."

"It seems to me it'll be kind of hard for anything to miss that goddamn gut you got, Turner," Earl stated as the rest of the men on the bench broke out laughing.

Before the anger rising in Turner's eyes could explode, Earl reached over and took the jug out of the man's hand. He knew from past experience that the store owner would take the jug back inside and not give any away if he thought for a moment that they were trying to make fun of him. Turner liked to talk. It made him feel important, and the only way he could hold an audience was to furnish the free whiskey. As long as the whiskey lasted, they would listen to his pompous sermons about other people.

Earl used one hand to push back the red-eyed store owner, while with the other he turned up the jug and took a big swig out of it.

While this was going on, the people still inside the bus peered out the windows at the strange looking hillbillies. Of course the men on the porch knew they were being watched, and many came into town at just the times the bus arrived so that they could strut and pose in front of the foreigners. Anyone who didn't live near them was considered either a Yankee or a foreigner. Very rarely would one of the passengers get out of the bus and stretch his legs in the strange little town.

It was something old man Turner had never imagined, that the group of men loitering on his porch drove away potential customers. The people who might have gotten off and bought some candy or a paperback novel lost their desire after one look at the hangers-on. The group of men smelled of trouble. Anything was better than nothing, and whatever broke the boredom was considered fun.

As the bus driver came out of the general store, the sheriff came out beside him. The sheriff was stooped over from age, and his face had lines and wrinkles that matched his whiskey-ravaged bloodshot eyes. Some of the people on the bus let out sighs of relief at the sight of the sheriff and bus driver. They knew it wouldn't be long now before they would be away from this country town.

"Well, Ed," the driver said to the sheriff, "maybe I'll see you nex' week when I'm due back through here. Anyhow, I'll tell Marge I saw you," he said, referring to his wife, who also happened to be the sheriff's only child.

The loitering men fell silent, listening with the hope of picking up some idle gossip—something they could pass on to the people in the backwoods who didn't come to town often because they were too busy trying to earn a living out of the farms they worked. Only the shiftless, lazy good-for-nothings hung out on the porch daily.

Two men started bear wrestling as the bus driver raced his motor once before slipping it into gear and pulling away. The other men let out loud yells, anything that might draw a fleeting moment of attention to themselves.

"By God, Sonny-Boy, there must have been an accident over at y'all's place or somethin'?" the sheriff inquired.

"Why hell, naw. I can't cotton to why you'd say that, Sheriff," Sonny-Boy answered, as his eyes followed the now fast-moving bus. In another moment it would be taking the right-hand turn and disappearing. For some reason, Sonny always felt funny whenever he saw the bus leave. Maybe it was because of his dream. He had never told anybody, but it was his ambition to one day take a ride on that bus. Just to see where it went. In all his twenty-five years, he had never been over twenty-five miles away from his home. He had been deep in the swamp, but that didn't count. He had never seen a large city, other than on television. And television was a rarity. To see one, you had to visit one of the large farmers on one of the plantations, then hope he invited you to watch the electronic miracle.

"Why would I say it?" Sheriff Ed Bradford repeated. "Why, it's just common sense, that's all. Your brothers Zeke and Jamie, they ain't here. This is the first time I can remember they missed the bus comin'. Why, I can't even recall when they did that before. You boys always come out of that swamp, rain or shine, once a week for the comin' of the bus."

Seeing his younger brother getting in deeper than he wanted him to, Jake, the oldest brother, spoke up. "Them boys got a big order on some 'gator hides, Ed," Jake stated, as he removed a bag of tobacco from his shirt pocket and began to roll a cigarette with one hand. "Yeah, them boys ought to be knee deep in 'gator shit 'bout this time of day. They been gone since last night, so I figure they made a good kill and stayed in the swamps skinning," the tall blond man stated, slowly rubbing the scar on his left cheek.

The sheriff had stated many times that, if you want-

ed to find out if the Jones boys were lying, get Jake
to tell it and watch and see if he didn't rub that old
scar of his. If he did, you could bet your roll he was
tellin' one of the damnedest lies of his life!

The departure of the bus was not only watched by
the men on the porch, but Jefferson watched it leave
with a feeling of dread. Perspiration broke out on his
forehead as he whirled around to Henrietta.

"You little fool!" he yelled angrily. "If'n you'd only
listened, but you can't listen 'cause you done went
and got too smart!"

"I'm sorry, Mr. Jefferson, that you feel that way. I
was going to ask you to help me with my bags until
we ran into George, but that's all right. I don't want
to impose on you any longer," she stated arrogantly.
Before she could snatch up her bags, he reached out
and held one.

"Listen, child," he said, and his voice sounded so
hurt and serious that she stopped to listen. "You yourself know that something must have happened or
George would be here by now. Nothing natural would
have held that boy up, so somethin' happened. Now,
I could offer you my room to stay in if you want it,
but it'd be another week now before the bus comes
back." She started to speak, but he held up his hand.
"Them honkies got somethin' in mind, child, 'bout
you. I say they been talkin' 'bout it ever since last
night. Now, I'm too old. I'd only hold you back. But
what you got to do is act like you leavin' for y'all's
place, then when you get out on the road, cut across
the field and run for Massah Wilson's plantation. Once

you get there, ain't no white trash goin' pester you, 'cause Massah Wilson don't allow them on his property."

Henrietta listened quietly, then asked, "You don't want to help me carry my bags home, then?"

Jefferson shook his head. "Gal, ain't you been hearing what I been sayin'? I can't help you out on that road when them night riders come down on us. Ain't nothin' I can do but die, and I just ain't ready for it yet. I'm askin' you to do what I say. Leave your bags with me, then take off like you goin' walk home. Without the bags slowin' you none, you might be able to get across the field before any of them realize you ain't going home. That's your only chance, child. The only one you got!"

Without another word, she pushed the bags toward him and started walking. Jefferson watched her go, praying she would do like he said. It would make the night riders mad, but just maybe it would hold them animals off. They'd have to think twice about raiding the farm, if she ever got home. They'd be scheming for the next week on how to get to her—maybe even puttin' it off until it was time for her departure. Then all old man Ben and George would have to do would be to figure out some way to get her to the bus without their being waylayed on the way. It could be done, even if they'd have to beg some of the other niggers from the plantations to come by and ride to town with her. That way, they would have a chance. The so-called night riders would think twice about tackling six or seven niggers armed with shotguns. But first things first. She had a chance, if she'd only realize her danger. Jefferson stood and watched until Henrietta was out of sight, then turned to observe what was happening across the street.

The two white men on the porch gave Henrietta a good ten-minute head start, just as Jefferson had hoped they would. Now all she had to do was follow his suggestion and everything would be all right. He stood in the same spot and watched the two white men walk past.

"Lord," he prayed, "this poo' nigga' ain't never asked for much, so please, Suh, just this time, let this one get away. Please, Lord, give this one a chance!"

2

HENRIETTA WATCHED CLOSELY as the bus moved quickly through Buckwater, Mississippi. The population of the small town was two hundred, not counting the blacks. The few houses they passed were actually shacks. It would have been more appropriate to have called it Shanty Town. The crudely-made outhouses could be seen in the rear of each dwelling.

The sight of the town made Henrietta sick. How she despised the place. She thought of her talented brother with his ability to pick things up by himself. She remembered sending him the book on advanced math, thinking he could never understand it without some kind of help. Yet, reading slowly, he had learned from

the book. If there were only some way of taking him
out when I left, she thought. But their grandfather pre-
sented a problem. If she could talk the old man into
leaving, then it could work. Once back in Atlanta,
Georgia, she could get an agency to help. Then her
dream of getting little George out of that swamp
would come true.

The very thought of the swamp resurrected her
hatred for the place. Hate wasn't the word. Loathing
was more like it. The swamp was a loathsome thing,
like the creepy, crawly creatures that lived there.
Henrietta shivered and stood up as the bus parked in
front of the white-walled drugstore.

In front of the drugstore was a homemade, gray-
colored bench. Every day it was filled with the various
white men who had tramped in from the farms and
shanties. The drugstore also served as the hardware
store and was one of only two places you could buy
your supplies. Next to it was the log cabin post office
and the jail house. The street ended with the only bar
and the other general store. That section was always
busy at night when the two town whores were there.

Henrietta stepped from the bus with her two suitcases and looked around for George. She had just
known that he would be there. Something must have
happened, but what? She walked slowly past the staring men and stopped at the edge of the wooden walk.
The rest of the way was a dirt road leading toward
the trail out of town. If George was coming, that was
the way he would come.

As Henrietta watched for George, she noticed old

man Jefferson waving at her. She figured she could get the old man to help her with the two suitcases she had brought with her. She gathered up her luggage and ran across the street to where Jefferson stood. She didn't notice the frowns on the white men's faces, but Jefferson saw it and read a warning in it.

As she came hurrying over, the old man said quickly, "Gal, get back on the bus! Hurry, if'n yo' don't wanna have trouble out of them there crackers, 'cause they been sittin' and waitin' for yo' all mornin'."

"Why, that's impossible. They had no way of knowing. I'm sure you're just imagining things, Mr. Jefferson," she said lightly, not even considering getting back on the bus.

Jefferson shook his head. "Gal, I ain't foolin' with you. Go on now and get back on the bus."

She decided she had better take a firm hand with him. She had become used to working with elderly people from a job she held near the college at the Martin Luther King convalescent center for the elderly. Old people had a bad habit of getting bossy in their old age. Now here was this fool trying to order her back on the bus after she had endured that bumpy overnight ride.

Henrietta wasn't very tall, but she had a way of carrying herself and walking proud. She was slim, on the border of being skinny, yet she filled out the brown pants outfit she wore to perfection. Proud and haughty, that was the opinion of the men who watched her with interest.

"By God," Sonny-Boy Jones began, "that fuckin'

bitch is still stuck-up as hell! Gets off the bus like she owns this here town, sees us sittin' here, then got the uppity not to speak!"

"Aw now, Sonny. What you expect?" the short, muscular Earl Mason stated. Earl didn't bat an eye as Sonny turned on him. He stared into Sonny's cold, fishlike pale blue eyes and continued. "The gal witnessed the death of her pa before she left, so why the hell should she speak to some of the people she thinks killed him?" The breeze blew Earl's hair down in his face. He took his hand and pushed the reddish mass back out of his brown eyes.

Old man Turner, the owner of the general store, came out the door carrying a jug. "Yeah," he began, drawing the word out, making sure he held everybody's attention before he began to speak. "That old black gal done filled out a little since leavin'. Looks like she been eatin' wherever she been."

As the group of men watched and waited, old man Turner took his time about uncorking the jug. Every eye on the porch followed his motion as he tilted the jug up, swinging it over his forearm for support, and let the furious, burning corn liquor run down his throat like water. When he brought the jug back down, he patted his huge belly.

"A'llll," Turner groaned, "that's how you can tell good likker. It hits you in the gut."

"It seems to me it'll be kind of hard for anything to miss that goddamn gut you got, Turner," Earl stated as the rest of the men on the bench broke out laughing.

Before the anger rising in Turner's eyes could explode, Earl reached over and took the jug out of the man's hand. He knew from past experience that the store owner would take the jug back inside and not give any away if he thought for a moment that they were trying to make fun of him. Turner liked to talk. It made him feel important, and the only way he could hold an audience was to furnish the free whiskey. As long as the whiskey lasted, they would listen to his pompous sermons about other people.

Earl used one hand to push back the red-eyed store owner, while with the other he turned up the jug and took a big swig out of it.

While this was going on, the people still inside the bus peered out the windows at the strange looking hillbillies. Of course the men on the porch knew they were being watched, and many came into town at just the times the bus arrived so that they could strut and pose in front of the foreigners. Anyone who didn't live near them was considered either a Yankee or a foreigner. Very rarely would one of the passengers get out of the bus and stretch his legs in the strange little town.

It was something old man Turner had never imagined, that the group of men loitering on his porch drove away potential customers. The people who might have gotten off and bought some candy or a paperback novel lost their desire after one look at the hangers-on. The group of men smelled of trouble. Anything was better than nothing, and whatever broke the boredom was considered fun.

As the bus driver came out of the general store, the sheriff came out beside him. The sheriff was stooped over from age, and his face had lines and wrinkles that matched his whiskey-ravaged bloodshot eyes. Some of the people on the bus let out sighs of relief at the sight of the sheriff and bus driver. They knew it wouldn't be long now before they would be away from this country town.

"Well, Ed," the driver said to the sheriff, "maybe I'll see you nex' week when I'm due back through here. Anyhow, I'll tell Marge I saw you," he said, referring to his wife, who also happened to be the sheriff's only child.

The loitering men fell silent, listening with the hope of picking up some idle gossip—something they could pass on to the people in the backwoods who didn't come to town often because they were too busy trying to earn a living out of the farms they worked. Only the shiftless, lazy good-for-nothings hung out on the porch daily.

Two men started bear wrestling as the bus driver raced his motor once before slipping it into gear and pulling away. The other men let out loud yells, anything that might draw a fleeting moment of attention to themselves.

"By God, Sonny-Boy, there must have been an accident over at y'all's place or somethin'?" the sheriff inquired.

"Why hell, naw. I can't cotton to why you'd say that, Sheriff," Sonny-Boy answered, as his eyes followed the now fast-moving bus. In another moment it would be taking the right-hand turn and disappearing. For some reason, Sonny always felt funny whenever he saw the bus leave. Maybe it was because of his dream. He had never told anybody, but it was his ambition to one day take a ride on that bus. Just to see where it went. In all his twenty-five years, he had never been over twenty-five miles away from his home. He had been deep in the swamp, but that didn't count. He had never seen a large city, other than on television. And television was a rarity. To see one, you had to visit one of the large farmers on one of the plantations, then hope he invited you to watch the electronic miracle.

"Why would I say it?" Sheriff Ed Bradford repeated. "Why, it's just common sense, that's all. Your brothers Zeke and Jamie, they ain't here. This is the first time I can remember they missed the bus comin'. Why, I can't even recall when they did that before. You boys always come out of that swamp, rain or shine, once a week for the comin' of the bus."

Seeing his younger brother getting in deeper than he wanted him to, Jake, the oldest brother, spoke up. "Them boys got a big order on some 'gator hides, Ed," Jake stated, as he removed a bag of tobacco from his shirt pocket and began to roll a cigarette with one hand. "Yeah, them boys ought to be knee deep in 'gator shit 'bout this time of day. They been gone since last night, so I figure they made a good kill and stayed in the swamps skinning," the tall blond man stated, slowly rubbing the scar on his left cheek.

The sheriff had stated many times that, if you want-

ed to find out if the Jones boys were lying, get Jake
to tell it and watch and see if he didn't rub that old
scar of his. If he did, you could bet your roll he was
tellin' one of the damnedest lies of his life!

The departure of the bus was not only watched by
the men on the porch, but Jefferson watched it leave
with a feeling of dread. Perspiration broke out on his
forehead as he whirled around to Henrietta.

"You little fool!" he yelled angrily. "If'n you'd only
listened, but you can't listen 'cause you done went
and got too smart!"

"I'm sorry, Mr. Jefferson, that you feel that way. I
was going to ask you to help me with my bags until
we ran into George, but that's all right. I don't want
to impose on you any longer," she stated arrogantly.
Before she could snatch up her bags, he reached out
and held one.

"Listen, child," he said, and his voice sounded so
hurt and serious that she stopped to listen. "You yourself know that something must have happened or
George would be here by now. Nothing natural would
have held that boy up, so somethin' happened. Now,
I could offer you my room to stay in if you want it,
but it'd be another week now before the bus comes
back." She started to speak, but he held up his hand.
"Them honkies got somethin' in mind, child, 'bout
you. I say they been talkin' 'bout it ever since last
night. Now, I'm too old. I'd only hold you back. But
what you got to do is act like you leavin' for y'all's
place, then when you get out on the road, cut across
the field and run for Massah Wilson's plantation. Once

you get there, ain't no white trash goin' pester you, 'cause Massah Wilson don't allow them on his property."

Henrietta listened quietly, then asked, "You don't want to help me carry my bags home, then?"

Jefferson shook his head. "Gal, ain't you been hearing what I been sayin'? I can't help you out on that road when them night riders come down on us. Ain't nothin' I can do but die, and I just ain't ready for it yet. I'm askin' you to do what I say. Leave your bags with me, then take off like you goin' walk home. Without the bags slowin' you none, you might be able to get across the field before any of them realize you ain't going home. That's your only chance, child. The only one you got!"

Without another word, she pushed the bags toward him and started walking. Jefferson watched her go, praying she would do like he said. It would make the night riders mad, but just maybe it would hold them animals off. They'd have to think twice about raiding the farm, if she ever got home. They'd be scheming for the next week on how to get to her—maybe even puttin' it off until it was time for her departure. Then all old man Ben and George would have to do would be to figure out some way to get her to the bus without their being waylayed on the way.

SPECIAL PREVIEW SECTION FEATURE

George Jackson was a "Swamp Man," born and bred in the dark watery woods of Mississippi. He was a gentle young man who turned as deadly as a

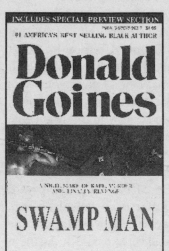

water moccasin after he saw what the four hill boys did to his sister. They caught her soon after she got off the bus, home from her first year of college. When they were through with her, she let her mind shut down, fearing to remember. Slipping through the swamps like a ghost, George stalked them, one by one, two by two....

No one knows the streets better than
Donald Goines

Check out his other books at:
www.kensingtonbooks.com